DO YOU DARE?

PUFFIN BOOKS

Published by the Penguin Group
Melbourne • London • New York • Toronto • Dublin
New Delhi • Auckland • Johannesburg • Beijing

Penguin Books Ltd, Registered Offices:
80 Strand, London WC2R 0RL, England
Published by Penguin Group (Australia), 2014

10 9 8 7 6 5 4 3 2 1

Cover and internal design by Tony Palmer
copyright © Penguin Group (Australia)
Cover illustrations copyright © Guy Shield
Printed and bound in Australia by McPherson's Printing Group,
Maryborough, Victoria

National Library of Australia
Cataloguing-in-Publication data available.
ISBN 978 0 14 330756 3

puffin.com.au

MIX
Paper from
responsible sources
FSC® C001695

The Publisher would like to thank Jocelyn Pride and the
boys from Scotch College, Melbourne, for their assistance
in providing feedback on this story.

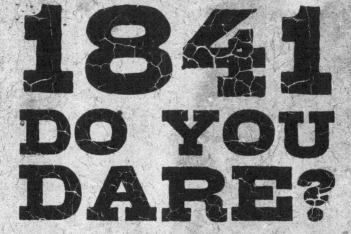

1841
DO YOU DARE?

THE BUSHRANGER'S BOYS

A. LLOYD

PUFFIN BOOKS

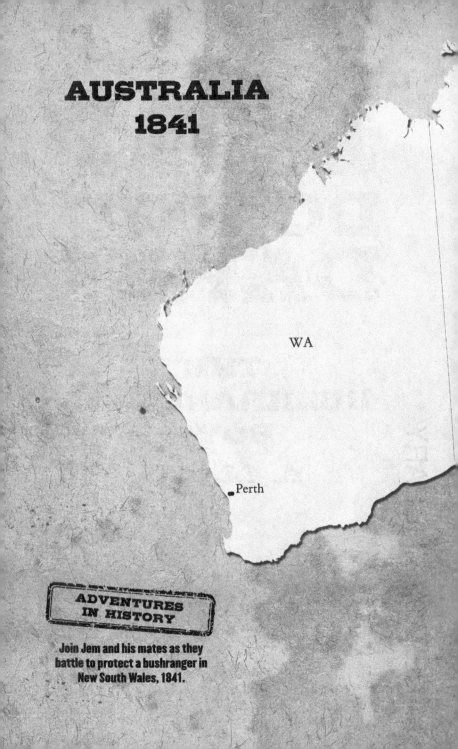

AUSTRALIA
1841

WA

• Perth

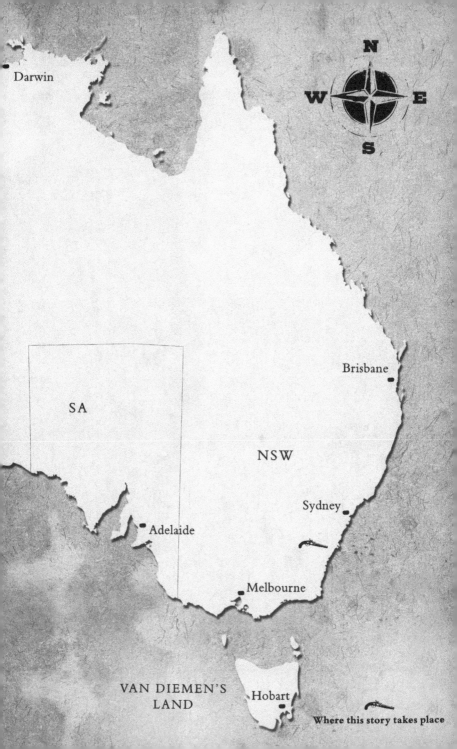

Darwin

N
W E
S

SA

Brisbane

NSW

Sydney

Adelaide

Melbourne

VAN DIEMEN'S
LAND

Hobart

Where this story takes place

I recognise the traditional Ngarigo owners of the Monaro plain, in southern New South Wales, where this book is set. The first theft in this story is really the takeover of their land by settlers.

Thank you to the Ngarigo women, the 'black powder' gun enthusiasts and the others who helped me write this book.

A. Lloyd

THE Sydney Gazette

William Westwood, alias Jackey Jackey, is still a ranger of the bush, and is said to be levying contributions between Bungendore and Maneroo Plains. Two gentlemen were robbed by this desperado a few days ago… The whole of the southern districts are kept in constant alarm by reports of the hellish doings of Westwood and his companions in blood and robbery…

12 JUNE, 1841

1

Jem gripped the money tight. He felt the hard edges of the silver coins in his palm. He waited with his dad. Their sheepdog, the Old Girl – lay warm across his feet. She chewed a piece of bark that had fallen from the roof.

Jem had always lived in this slab hut. His dad had built it, but it wasn't theirs. It belonged to Captain Ross. So did the sheep and the four miles of land in front of them. So did another run and the Station, twenty miles away. But today could change all that.

The money Jem held, knotted in a handkerchief, was their own. It had been saved penny by penny, year by year. Jem had gone without shoes to make up the last few shillings. That's why Jem's dad let him hold it. Ten whole pounds, it was. The price the Captain wanted for this run. Today the Captain was coming to get it. He had promised to sell them the land.

The Old Girl stopped chewing and began to growl. A minute later, Jem saw the Captain riding up the paddock. He had a quality horse. She had a white diamond on her face, a shiny coat and fast legs. For some reason, the Captain was also leading an old mare with a hide like a scrubbing brush. She wouldn't be a gift, that was for sure. Not from the Captain.

The Old Girl's hackles rose. Her ears flattened against her skull. She stood up and approached the Captain's horse warily, with a deep growling bark.

'Hush now,' said Jem's dad. He took off his hat and rubbed the brim with his thumb. He was afraid of the Captain too, Jem thought.

'Call off your damn dog,' Captain Ross ordered.

Jem's dad whistled. The Old Girl backed up a few steps.

Captain Ross stayed on his horse. 'So you still want to buy this run?' he said.

Jem's dad nodded.

Captain Ross looked out over the paddocks. 'I've reconsidered,' he said.

Jem's dad turned his hat around and around. He looked at the Captain.

'I'll offer you a fair deal,' the Captain said. 'Thirty pounds – and you can keep half the sheep.'

Thirty pounds! Jem's dad didn't have thirty pounds – would never have thirty pounds. He already worked until he was too knackered to eat. Captain Ross knew that, of course. That would be why he'd put the price up. Jem wanted to throw the bag of money in his face and smack his stuck-up nose.

Another growl rumbled in the Old Girl's throat.

Jem's dad gripped his hat like he was holding it together. 'I've been an honest worker for you all this while,' he said. 'You can't take less?'

Captain Ross twitched his black moustache. 'In my book,' he said, 'once a thief, always a thief. You might be free, but you've done no more than make up what you owe.'

What about the money we saved? Jem wanted to say. But he saw the Captain's hand curl in a fist around the gun strapped to the front of his saddle. It was an expensive musket, with swirls of brass in the stock. It was as if the Captain was saying: do you really want to argue with a man like me?

Captain Ross shrugged his shoulders. 'I will make you an offer,' he said. 'I need more men at the homestead, now that I can't get new convicts. Your son is tall for his age. I'll employ him on half wages.'

Jem's dad put a hand on his son's shoulder. 'Jem's a good boy,' he said. 'He's good with animals. I was planning to keep him with me.'

'These are my animals, and I don't need him here,' said the Captain. 'He can work in my stables.'

Jem's dad rubbed his hand slowly over his face. It gave Jem a bad feeling in his guts – his dad usually did that when a lamb wasn't going to make it. His dad bent down and undid his boot laces. Jem saw the old red scars that ringed his father's ankles, from the convict shackles Captain Ross had once locked him in.

'Dad?' Was his dad agreeing? Did this mean Jem was leaving?

Jem's dad took off his boots and gave them to Jem. 'Better wear these, son. You don't want the Captain's horses busting your feet.' He took the handkerchief with the money.

Jem put on the boots. They didn't fit right.

The whole day didn't fit right. Jem didn't want to go anywhere.

Jem's dad put his hand on his son's back, and pushed him gently towards the Captain. Jem clomped forward awkwardly. He climbed onto the old mare.

The Old Girl watched with her head on one side like she couldn't work it out. Jem would have liked to kiss her goodbye, but not in front of the Captain.

Captain Ross spoke to Jem. His long black sideburns underlined his jaw. 'You'd better not follow your father's bad ways,' he warned, 'or you'll come to nothing. I'll make sure of it.'

Jem was silent, because he felt like nothing he said would make any difference. He felt as if his life had been taken off him and stuffed inside the Captain's saddlebags.

The Captain flicked his riding whip, the diamond-faced filly flicked her hooves, and the mare shambled down the track after them, carrying Jem away.

Jem saw the Old Girl look from him to his dad. She began to bark. When Jem reached the rise, the last place he could see home from, she broke away. She pelted across the paddock to Jem. The Captain's horse skipped sideways and nearly threw him. The Captain cursed.

'Go home, Girl,' Jem told her.

But she wouldn't. She came at the horses, barking. She was trying to round him up, Jem knew, as if he was a stray sheep that should return to his pen.

Before Jem realised, the Captain had taken his musket from the saddle. He cocked the trigger, and lifted the weapon to his shoulder.

'No!' Jem shouted.

Captain Ross didn't listen. His finger moved on the trigger. Smoke and noise exploded around them. Both the horses jumped. Jem didn't try to stay on. He hit the ground hard, stumbled to his feet and ran to the Old Girl.

She was lying on her side when Jem got to her. He saw a long shiver go through her body, head to tail. Her four paws quivered. Then they stopped.

Slowly, Jem turned to face the Captain. Jem was shaking.

'I hate you,' he said.

'Why should I care?' Captain Ross replied. 'Get back on that horse.'

Jem sat like a lump of wood while the horses plodded on. He kept imagining the Old Girl was following them.

When the horses stopped, Jem noticed they had reached the place where the wattles closed in along the river. He had heard of a stickup here by a bushranger, not long before. He saw the Captain's fingers hook over his musket barrel again. Jem tensed.

The Captain looked up and down the river. He turned and spoke to Jem. 'When we're over the creek, we're back on my land,' he said.

His land, thought Jem. Such a lot of land. How did he come to have all that, and Jem have nothing? Not even a dog.

The horses tilted down the bank, their hooves slipping on the icy mud. The Captain's horse surged into the river. Jem's horse stopped dead in the mud. Jem gave her a prod in the flanks. But she wouldn't budge. She shook her head as if she didn't like walking all this way with a strange boy on top. Jem didn't like it either.

The Captain stopped on the far side and looked back again.

'Daisy!' he said sharply. 'Move.'

That was when Jem saw the man up ahead. He wasn't hiding in the bushes. He was leaning against a gum tree. He waved at Jem. But it wasn't a 'g'day' wave. More of a 'stay back'.

What's more, he had a red scarf tied over his face. In his right hand was a slim dark shape – a pistol. It was the bushranger.

The man was signalling him to dismount, Jem

realised. He slithered to the ground.

Captain Ross still had his back to the path ahead. He raised his voice at Jem. 'What the deuce! Get back on the horse, boy.'

Jem didn't. He stood perfectly still.

The bushranger nodded at Jem. He lowered his pistol so it was pointing at Captain Ross.

'Sir!' he called.

Captain Ross turned around. Jem couldn't see the Captain's face, but he saw his back and shoulders stiffen.

'Stand or I'll blow your head off,' the stranger ordered.

With the pistol already aimed at him, Captain Ross didn't have a chance to take out his musket. He couldn't do anything except get slowly out of the saddle.

'Step away from the horse and turn out your pockets,' the bushranger told the Captain. His eyes fixed on Jem over the top of the scarf. 'Boy – don't you move.'

Jem wasn't going to. As long as the gun wasn't pointed at him, he would be all right. He owned nothing worth stealing. He'd already lost the best thing in his life that day.

The Captain took a shilling and sixpence out of one trouser pocket, and a handkerchief out of the other. Then he held his hands in the air.

'That's lightweight for a gentleman like you,' said the bushranger. 'You've forgotten your coat pockets.'

Captain Ross lowered his hands reluctantly. His outside coat pockets did have more in them – coins, a ring of keys and a short knife.

'Put them on the ground.' The bushranger still held his gun level. 'I'm waiting for your breast pocket. Either you empty it, or I'll put a hole in it for you.'

The Captain gritted his teeth. He pulled a banknote from the inside of his coat. Jem watched it flutter onto the pile. He knew banknotes could be worth a lot, even more than thirty pounds.

Seeing the money on the ground made his heart beat faster.

The bushranger wasn't finished. 'Why not take off your nice velvet coat?' he said. His voice sounded to Jem as if he was smiling. 'I could do with new trousers too.'

Captain Ross's eyes bulged and his face went red. He undressed right there. Lucky for him, he was wearing long underwear. He looked a lot less like a Captain in tight grey smalls, Jem thought. More like a featherless emu.

'Now leave the filly, and walk a hundred yards ahead,' ordered the bushranger.

Captain Ross walked up the path, past the bushranger, with his hands held in the air. The bushranger's gun followed the Captain the whole time.

When Captain Ross was far enough away, the bushranger stuffed his pistol into his belt. He walked down the path towards Jem and the horses. Jem's palms were sweaty. He wondered if he should run. Jem was no slouch at running, but a shot would beat him. Like the one that got the Old Girl. He made himself stand still.

The bushranger didn't seem too concerned about Jem. Instead he brushed dirt off the coat and put it on. He folded the silver coins inside the banknote. Then he rolled everything up in the Captain's trousers and stuffed them in the Captain's saddlebags. The man was so close Jem could see a small blue tattoo on the back of his hand.

The bushranger mounted Captain Ross's horse. He tossed Daisy's lead rein to Jem.

'It's been a pleasure doing business with you,' he said. Jem could swear he was laughing under his scarf. The bushranger rode off, with the Captain's cash and the Captain's clothes.

Jem thought it served the iron-hearted Captain right. Secretly, he wished the bushranger had been rougher with Captain Ross. Jem could hardly believe the robbery had been so easy. As he watched the bushranger go, he admired his nerve, as well as the money in his bags.

2

After that, Captain Ross rode Daisy and made Jem walk to Ross Vale Station. All the way, Jem wished he could tell his dad what had happened. He wished he could be there to bury his dog. But he knew it could be a long time before he saw his dad again.

The Station sat in the middle of a flat paddock, not far from the creek. There were so many buildings it looked like a town to Jem. Lots of people were in the yard too: eight or nine stockmen were washing their hands, a woman in an apron passed a bucket to a boy, and a group of Aborigines stood by a side door.

They were almost all strangers to Jem. And

they were all staring at him. Jem wanted to turn his back and walk right home. But his dad's heavy boots had turned to stone, and he had blisters that hurt with every step.

Then Jem realised the people weren't staring at him – they were staring at the Captain, stripped of his fine stuff. The Captain's jaw had set like a rock. His face was so red you could light a match on it. Jem wanted to laugh.

'Sir?' A man stepped forward to hold Daisy's reins. Jem recognised him as Mr Blain. He was the Captain's overseer, second in charge, and too friendly. Jem's dad said he was the sort of man who'd slap you on the back then dob you in to the master. Here Jem would have to work for him.

The Captain got off Daisy without a word. He pulled his riding gloves off, finger by finger, and tossed them at the overseer.

'Get rid of the blacks from my house, Mr Blain,' he said. He handed his whip to Mr Blain too.

The Captain went to his big front door. As it opened, Jem caught a glimpse of a long corridor with floorboards – not dirt – and painted walls. The windows had clear glass in them. It was a very fine house, like the Captain's coat and horse and gun. Or at least, like the Captain's coat, horse and gun had been, while they were still his, Jem thought. Captain Ross slammed the door behind him.

Mr Blain swung the Captain's whip and cracked it over the heads of the Aborigines. Jem saw them flinch.

'You no work,' Mr Blain said, 'we no give tobacco. No give flour.'

The black men shrugged their shoulders under their possum-skin cloaks and backed away.

Mr Blain shook the whip at them. Then he smiled at Jem. He had long yellow teeth like an old sheep's.

'Tell us what happened, sonny,' he said.

'We were crossing the creek, a few miles

back,' Jem mumbled. He wasn't used to talking to strangers. 'A man with a gun bailed us up.'

'A bushranger!' The other boy and the stockmen gathered around them. The boy was about the same age as Jem, but smaller. He had a whopper of a nose, though. 'Is that how the Captain got his new suit of clothes?' he said.

The stockmen laughed.

'Alfie!' The woman glared. The boy went quiet.

'Which way did the villain go?' the overseer wanted to know.

'Back north,' Jem said.

'Towards Bungendore and the Sydney Road? Let's hope he runs into the troopers,' Mr Blain said. 'If he'd gone for the hills we'd have to turn out after him.'

'No more of this talk,' the woman said. 'Dinner is waiting.'

After dinner, Mr Blain led Jem across the dark yard. He pointed out his own hut, next to the cottage of Mrs Goods – the cook – and her boy Alfie. He led Jem to the farm hands' lean-to, up against the brick stables.

Mr Blain held an old blanket out to him. 'I bet the Captain rues the day he brought you in,' he said. He winked as if it was a joke. 'Not a good start to your employment, hey?'

Jem didn't find that funny. It had been a hell of a start, and it was the Captain's fault.

Jem took an empty bunk. He wrapped the blanket tight around him, but his feet were cold as a lazy man's dinner. The Captain's horses had better sleeping quarters than his men. Jem's thoughts were even colder than his feet. He missed home. He hated the Captain for putting up the price of the land. He wasn't happy his dad had let the Captain take him away. And he didn't like remembering his dad standing there, uselessly twisting his hat, while their dog... Jem tried not to think about her anymore.

Jem did not want to be like his dad. Being miserable and beaten was hard to take. Being angry was better. Jem thought the bushranger had taught him something. He had shown Jem that you didn't have to let the Captain get his way. If you dared.

Jem stared into the darkness. He heard the soft stamping and huffing of horses from inside the stable, through a hole where a brick was missing.

There was another sound too, higher. What was it? A whimper?

The other men had gone to sleep. There was the noise again – it sounded almost like a little kid. Jem didn't stop to think whether it was his business. He got up. With the blanket wrapped around him he crept to the stables.

A shaft of grey moonlight slanted through the hole. The corners of the stable were pits of darkness. The sound came again, from one of the corners. *Yip, yip, aa-oo.*

Jem felt his way forward. The pile of straw was warm under his feet. A creature had been lying here.

Ow. He stubbed his toe on a wooden barrel. Then he felt a damp nose sniffing around his ankle. It was a dog. Jem stood still. He was new to the Station so he'd better let the dog get to know him. He held out a fist for it to sniff.

Yip, yip. The whimpering noise started again, and it wasn't the dog at his feet. Jem thought it was in front of him, inside the barrel. He couldn't see. He felt for the edge and leaned over, reaching inside. His fingers went down through air until they brushed something warm. Then a hot tongue rasped his hand – a puppy.

'How did you get in here, silly critter? Quit licking a minute, will you?' Jem put both hands in the barrel. His fingers went under the puppy's belly where the skin was bare and soft. 'Don't wriggle!' The puppy squirmed madly, wagging its whole behind. Puppies rated higher than people and even higher than money to Jem. Unlike money they grew by themselves, and unlike most people they loved you back.

'There you go.' He put it down beside its mother. The mother's tail banged happily on his legs. She turned a few circles in the straw, and settled down. The puppy scrambled over Jem's feet. Jem heard it scuffling in the straw. Then it scrambled back over his feet again and pulled at his trouser leg with its teeth.

'Hey! You want me to stay, do you?' Jem sat down. He scooped the puppy into his lap. The mother didn't seem to mind. Jem leaned back into a mound of straw. The puppy wasn't a newborn — maybe a couple of months old, Jem guessed. He stroked it and smelt its rich, furry smell. It was the same good smell as the Old Girl. Jem squeezed his eyes shut against his tears. The puppy sighed. Jem tucked the blanket around them both. He could feel the puppy breathing in and out against his belly. The warmth of the mother lay over his feet.

Jem wasn't alone anymore and he wasn't so cold.

'Puppy,' he whispered, 'I'm going to beat the Captain, somehow.'

He fell asleep.

3

Jem woke up next morning to puppy breath on his face.

'Ugh, stink!' he grumbled.

The puppy perked its ears and looked extremely pleased. Nose-to-tail it was about as long as Jem's arm. But it still had a roly-poly tummy and big puppy paws, which it plonked on Jem's hair. 'Ouch!' Jem got his hair loose.

He had his first day of work at the station ahead of him. The best thing for him to do was knuckle down, earn his money, and wait for his chance against the Captain.

The stable door opened. An arm of light reached for them. Jem saw the puppy's fur was the colour of brown sugar and cream.

The overseer came in. 'You're in here?'

'Yes, sir,' said Jem. 'I was cold.'

'Suit yourself.' Mr Blain shrugged. He pointed to the wall. 'Get me the old saddle. That damn outlaw took the good one yesterday. The master is going to ride the chestnut to Bungendore after breakfast,' he explained. 'He's written a report about the bushranger. He'll send it to the government in Sydney.'

Jem took the heavy saddle down. He noticed that the leather girth strap, which went under the horse's belly, was worn and stretched. Jem helped as he was told. But he thought about how the strap would break if it was stretched enough – and how the Captain would tumble off his high horse. He would like to be there to see it happen.

That was the beginning of Jem 'learning the ropes', as Mr Blain put it. What Jem actually learnt was horse manure: how to shovel it, lug it, scrub it away, then feed the horses to make a new pile of it. On the quiet, he fiddled with the girth strap, rubbing it thinner and thinner.

He had the horses and the dogs for company. The pup thought Jem's job was a big game. She jumped on the shovel and bit the handle every time Jem lowered it. After a few days, the shovel had a lot of chew marks. The puppy chewed plenty of poo too. She also adored water. When Jem didn't watch out, she knocked the water bucket over trying to climb into it. Then the stable floor got wet as well as pooey.

She was fun, but Jem missed his dad and his home. And the Old Girl.

Quite often, the boy Alfie came past and waved. He sometimes hung around the yard, until his mother called him. Jem ignored him. Alfie seemed to be part of Captain Ross's house, like Mr Blain, and Jem didn't want to talk to him.

The Captain came back from Bungendore,

without losing his clothes this time. He didn't say anything about the bushranger. Jem thought the outlaw must be a long way off by now.

As he returned to the main house, Captain Ross dropped a riding glove at the stable door. Jem saw it there, lying in the muck. One finger was curled up, like the glove was beckoning. Jem decided to ignore it. The Captain could come back and get his own glove. If he couldn't look after his stuff, then he owned too much of it.

The puppy saw it too. She picked it up with her needle-sharp teeth and shook it so the fingers slapped around her face.

Jem laughed. Daisy put her head over her stall and snorted.

'Go girl!' Jem said, leaning on his shovel.

The pup stood on the glove and clamped her teeth around a button. *Pop!* It came off. She bounced across the stable floor, found it, and slurped it up with her pink tongue. End of button, thought Jem.

She did the same thing all over again for the second button. Except this time it came off, bounced on her bottom, and she chased her tail in circles trying to find it.

Jem laughed and laughed, like he hadn't done since coming to Ross Vale. Until he realised that the Captain and Mr Blain were in the doorway, watching him.

The Captain frowned at Jem. 'I hired you to work, not –'

'Play,' Jem waited for him to say.

But the puppy ran over to the Captain with his glove in her mouth. She sat down, ears up, tail beating, inviting him to join in.

The Captain focused on the glove. 'What the deuce!' he said angrily. He bent down to take his glove, but of course the puppy sank her teeth in harder and pulled.

The overseer stepped forward and picked her up. 'Let me deal with it, sir,' he said.

Mr Blain prised the glove out of her mouth.

It was only slightly torn.

'In the river,' said the Captain. 'Tomorrow.'

Jem thought it was a waste to chuck away a glove like that, only because it had been in a dog's mouth.

The Captain turned to Jem. 'You should respect other people's property. I'm not having convict habits here.' He pulled a face, as if Jem were a sheep rotten with scab. 'You will work closer to the house, where Mrs Goods will keep an eye on you,' he said. 'In the scullery. You can share a bed with her son, instead of lying in the straw like an animal.'

Jem hated the Captain telling him what to do. He didn't want to leave the dogs and horses. He didn't want someone else to work in the stable and find the worn strap before it broke and tipped the Captain off his horse. He certainly didn't want to work in the scullery. The scullery was the outhouse where the pots were scrubbed and stored. It should be the job of a scullery maid.

But Ross Vale didn't have many women.

Mrs Goods was not impressed either when Jem went to the kitchen. She crossed her arms.

'What was the man thinking?' she said. 'I ask for a girl, so he brings me another boy. Really!'

When everyone had eaten that night, Mrs Goods lifted a kettle of hot water off the stove. 'Follow me,' she told Jem.

The scullery was a roof and a few boards around a splintery bench, with an iron tub and a wire brush. Beside the tub were piles and piles of dirty plates and pots.

'The blue-and-white dinner service is from China. The silver is English,' Mrs Goods said, in a respectful voice, like she was introducing the Queen. 'If any of them is not spotless, you'll do the lot again.'

Five plates later, Jem heaved a sigh. The wind blew through gaps in the boards and froze his wet knuckles. He had another fifty things to wash. Horse crap he could handle, but not fancy china.

'Bloody hell,' he said.

'Don't say that so loud!'

Jem looked around. Alfie stood at the scullery door. 'The Captain won't stand for swearing.'

'The Captain doesn't own my voice, does he?' Jem replied. He turned his back on Alfie and scrubbed a handful of spikey cutlery.

He scrubbed too hard and dropped a fork on his big toe. It hurt. Worse, because it landed on the dirt floor, he had to wash it again.

'Fork it!' he said.

Alfie laughed. 'I haven't heard that one before.'

'Nobody can say it's swearing then, can they?'

Alfie grinned. He had a big smile, to match his nose, and big crooked teeth. 'Where are you from?'

'Twenty miles away, near Bungendore,' Jem answered.

'You're not a convict then.' Alfie looked relieved. 'Ma won't let me hang about with convicts. She thinks they're bad. But now you're here I can talk to you.'

Jem didn't tell Alfie that his dad had been a 'government man'. Or that Jem was not keen to talk. Alfie would get that message soon enough.

But when Jem didn't reply, Alfie reached for the cloth at the end of the bench. He picked up one of the wet dishes and swirled the cloth over it.

Jem didn't think he wanted help from Alfie. He thought Alfie might be a bit wet, a bit of a mother's boy. 'Did your ma tell you to help me?' he asked.

Alfie shook his head. 'I thought, if we get this done, you can join in lessons at night.'

Jem didn't want to join Mrs Goods' lessons.

'We're reading *The Life of Nelson*,' said Alfie enthusiastically.

'Yeah?' said Jem. He'd never read anything.

'You know – Horatio Nelson, hero of the British navy – cannons, cutlasses, fighting the Frenchies. "England expects that every man shall do his duty!"' Alfie saluted. 'That stuff. It's good. So I came to help you get done quick.'

Nelson sounded all right, thought Jem. Shame it was a book. Maybe Alfie might be all right too. He was the first person at the Station to do something good for Jem.

'How about this then?' Jem challenged Alfie: 'We'll play slaps.' It was a game Jem played with his dad – you had to whack the other person's hands without them getting yours.

'With these,' said Jem. He picked up two big metal spoons. 'First to ten hits wins. If I win, you scrub the pots.'

Alfie got a spoon and weighed it in his hand. 'If I win, you help with my project,' he said.

'What's that?' said Jem.

'A secret,' said Alfie.

Jem wondered about Alfie's secret. But he

didn't expect to lose. He was bigger and stronger than Alfie.

'Deal,' he said.

'Right. Spare no quarter!' said Alfie.

Jem and Alfie went at each other hard and fast. Jem's blows were harder, but Alfie's were faster. At the end, both of them had bleeding knuckles. Neither of them admitted they hurt.

The score was 10–8, in Alfie's favour. Jem had to admit that Alfie was not a soppy mama's boy.

Alfie held out his right hand to Jem. 'Mates?' he offered.

Jem wasn't sure. The only real mate he'd had till now was his dad, who wasn't like Alfie at all. His dad was hardened and grey, like the wood slabs of their hut. He talked about as much as the boards did, especially compared to Alfie. But Jem was in a new place now. He'd lost the company of the animals, and maybe he needed a new mate if he was going to get his own back against the Captain. He held out his stinging hand.

'Mates,' he agreed.

'Huzzah!' said Alfie, and they shook on it.

Then Jem tackled the pots. He still hated washing up, but it wasn't so bad having Alfie there, rattling on about Nelson and navy battles.

4

Next morning Alfie was fidgety as a foal. Mrs Goods wanted them to go across the paddocks and pick up firewood, so Jem hitched Daisy to the cart. He called for the pup in the stable, to take her along, but she didn't show up. He hoped she wasn't stuck somewhere again.

Out in the paddocks, Jem loaded up enough dry timber for a week. Alfie didn't pick up one single branch. Instead he mucked about collecting a stack of dried cowpats.

'How about you pull your weight, Alfie.' Jem was annoyed.

'Teamwork,' said Alfie. 'We need these too.'

'What for?' Jem wasn't going to eat damper cooked in them.

Alfie grinned. 'You'll see. I've got something to show you – my project.' He pointed to a big hill, covered in bush, a mile or two away. 'Up there, on the neighbour's land. But first –'

He put his fingers to his lips and whistled like a bird. The same bird call replied from down by the creek.

'Must be a lyrebird there,' Jem said.

Alfie just laughed. A minute later he said, 'Here comes your lyrebird.'

An Aboriginal boy walked towards them. He was wearing half a dirty blanket pinned together at the shoulder with a bone, galah feathers in his hair, and nothing else except a smile.

'This is Tommy,' Alfie said. 'My other friend. The bird call is our secret signal. Tommy knows a lot of interesting things. The Captain made him live in the scullery for a while so he speaks English, as well as his language. Tommy, this is my mate, Jem.'

Jem had met Aborigines before, in Bungendore and when they helped his dad wash sheep. His dad said there used to be lots more of them in the early days when he'd first come to the Maneroo. Jem didn't know Tommy though. They looked at each other. Jem was not quick to make friends; maybe Tommy wasn't either.

'You gone deaf, Mr Alfie?' Tommy said. 'Every time I whistle – nothing.'

'It's my mother,' said Alfie. 'She's been worried about William Westwood, the bushranger on the loose. She wouldn't let me go out by myself. Tell him, Jem, about the stickup.'

Jem explained briefly, while Tommy walked along with them.

'You should have seen him in his smalls!'

Alfie laughed. But Tommy didn't see what was so funny. Probably, Jem thought, because he didn't wear underwear himself.

At the bottom of the hill, Alfie began to look over his shoulder all the time, as if the bushranger was after them.

'We've got to leave Daisy here,' he said. He tied the horse to a wattle and scooped up the cowpats. Then he lowered his voice. 'You mustn't let anyone know we've gone past the Captain's land. It's trespassing.'

Jem did not care whose land it was if it wasn't his. But it clearly bothered Alfie, so he must have a good reason for coming here, Jem thought.

Jem followed the other boys up. The bush got thicker. The hill got steeper and rockier. Jem puffed to keep up. Tommy loped along in front. Jem wished Tommy wasn't there. He didn't like being the latecomer, the tag-along of the group.

Near the top, a crown of rocks stood out above the trees. Jem craned his neck. The rocks were angled over the boys' heads – too high and too steep to climb.

'This way,' said Tommy, looking back at Jem. Alfie crawled first into a big bush with a lot of scratchy twigs.

The branches flicked back in Jem's face. This had better be worth it, he thought.

At the end of a wallaby track, a big kettle on a rope hung down the rock face. The kettle had a hole in the bottom, and no lid. Jem looked up through the rusty hole to the blue sky.

'Good thing no one wants a cup of tea,' he said.

A ladder also leaned against the rock. It was a pretty strange ladder – not one single piece of wood was sawed square or straight. Bent nails stuck out in painful places.

'We made it on our own,' said Alfie, obviously proud. 'I mean – it's not tiptop, cos it was the first thing I made, and nobody else knew so I couldn't ask for help, but, well…' Alfie stopped. He looked at Jem. 'What do you reckon?'

Jem reckoned it was all a bit crazy. 'Does it

work?' He examined the ladder doubtfully.

'Of course.' Alfie dumped the cow pats in the kettle. Then he climbed up the ladder like he'd done it a hundred times before.

So did Tommy. At the top he called, 'Come on.'

Jem didn't like Tommy telling him what to do. But because he wasn't going to be beaten, he climbed up too – carefully, watching for nails. The ladder ended at a rock platform, nestled into the crown.

'Welcome to our fort,' said Alfie. 'Now we can pull up the drawbridge.' Alfie heaved on a piece of rope tied to the top rung of the ladder. Once the ladder was up, nobody else could get in.

Smart, thought Jem.

That wasn't the only contraption Alfie had made in his project. In the middle was a strange two-ended sling, on a post. It looked like a catapult. There was also a *goongee*, a shelter built like the Aboriginal ones with sheets of bark.

'Tommy showed me how to do that,' Alfie said.

'Easy.' Tommy shrugged.

Jem thought it must have taken Alfie and Tommy days or weeks to do all this. Jem had helped his dad knock up sheep pens and other things. But he had never seen, or even thought of, anything like this.

Jem sniffed. Despite the breeze, the place had a slight pong about it. That was because of a man-high pile of cowpats on one side. When Jem saw that, he laughed.

'Alfie,' he said. 'You've built yourselves a giant crock of sh–'

'You don't need to bloody swear,' said Alfie. He crossed his arms and turned his face away.

Tommy touched Jem on the arm. 'You make him feel bad, maybe,' he said softly.

Jem had to admit Tommy was most likely right, and Alfie's fort was too good to be sneered at.

'Crock of gold, Alf,' he said, as an apology. 'I meant crock of gold. You could keep a stash of loot here, if you were a bushranger. This place is trumps.'

'We can make it even better,' said Alfie. 'We can build fortifications.'

Jem and Tommy looked at him blankly. Alfie knew a lot of book words.

'Fortifications are things like walls and watchtowers,' Alfie explained. 'We can move these loose stones to make shooting slits.'

'Sounds all right,' agreed Jem. He was beginning to like Alfie's enthusiasm.

Tommy nodded. 'Do what you think, Mr Alfie.'

Jem and Tommy helped Alfie heave and push, until they had created a 'battlement'. That's what Alfie called it. It was a line of stones along the top rock, with narrow gaps between them. The boys lay on their stomachs and peered out.

Tommy had his head to one side, like he was listening.

'I can hear a *yarraman*, I reckon.'

'What's he mean?' Jem said to Alfie.

'A horse,' said Alfie. 'Must've been Daisy. I can't see anyone else out there.'

Alfie's fort was a great lookout. In front Jem could see along the green line of the creek to Ross Vale. Past that he thought he could see the shimmer of Lake George, in the direction of Bungendore and his dad's hut near Long Swamp. Behind them, southwards, was a dark ridge of mountainous bush, where white people never went.

'This is like a crow's nest,' Alfie said happily. 'We could be Nelson's crew. Or a troop of British soldiers, defending our position.'

Tommy was quietly singing in his own language.

Jem took a deep breath of wind and wattle and wide space. It was way better up here than stuck in the Captain's scullery.

'From here, it feels like all New South Wales is ours,' he said. 'I wish it was.'

Tommy raised his eyebrows as if he saw things differently.

'Well at least some of it should be mine.' Thirty pounds worth, Jem thought. Enough country for his dad and Jem and a decent mob of stock. That was Jem's dream. The wind was going to Jem's head. He'd never wanted to tell so many of his thoughts before.

'One day,' he said, 'I'm going to canter across the Maneroo on a shiny thoroughbred. As pretty as that filly the bushranger stole from the Captain. I'll whistle to my dog, and she'll round up a hundred head of fat cattle. Milkers, they'll be, so I can have cheese when I want.'

Tommy laughed. 'Cheese is whitefella tucker,' he said. '*Mumugandi* are better.'

'Those moths?' said Alfie.

'Ugh,' said Jem, although he'd never had them.

'You know, I don't want to be a settler,' Alfie said. 'I want to build machines. Like the engineers in Nelson's navy.'

Jem looked at Alfie like he was a new breed of animal. That was a funny thing to want. 'What would you do with machines out here?' he asked.

'Lots!' Alfie said. 'This trebuchet is a sort of war machine. They had them in English castles.' He pointed to the post with slings. 'You can really fire it, you know. Hey, Tommy,' Alfie propped himself on one elbow, 'what about you? What'll you do when you grow up?'

Tommy looked surprised. 'My people been here from the beginning,' he said. 'This all my people's country. We hunt, we sing, all that. I don't want to change nothing.' Tommy stopped and thought for a bit. 'But you whitefellas are here now...' He scratched his head and a couple of feathers floated from the curls of his hair. 'That Captain – he's no good.'

Jem agreed completely.

Tommy pointed below. 'And that man, he's trouble too.'

Jem saw Mr Blain trudging across the paddocks.

Tommy gave a fake grin, showing his teeth and gums like Mr Blain did. Jem laughed. He decided he liked Tommy after all.

Alfie didn't laugh. 'It's a shame about that puppy in the stable,' he said sadly.

'Real pretty little *mirigan*,' Tommy agreed.

'It stinks,' said Alfie.

Jem was offended for the puppy. 'So does this place!'

'I mean, getting rid of it,' said Alfie, watching Mr Blain. 'That's what stinks.'

'What?' said Jem.

'See the sack he's got? The Captain sold most of the puppies in the litter, but nobody wanted the last one. Mr Blain's probably taking it to the creek to drown it.'

Was that what the Captain meant when he was talking about 'in the river tomorrow'? Fear and fury surged through Jem.

'We can't let him!' Jem jumped down from the battlement, swung the ladder back into position, and hurried down.

'It's his puppy, Jem,' Alfie called after him.

'He doesn't want it,' Jem yelled back.

He guessed they were almost as close to the creek as the overseer. If he ran like wildfire he might get to the water before Mr Blain did.

Then what? Maybe Jem could buy the pup, with his wages that hadn't been paid yet, or even earned yet. Or he could bail up the overseer like a bushranger. Or they would… he didn't know what they'd do. But he would not let the Captain's man kill the puppy. Not this dog too.

He could hear Alfie and Tommy racing after him. The three of them leaped over rocks and slithered on loose stones, in a scramble to the bottom of the hill.

'He won't let us keep it,' Alfie puffed.

'Don't be a yelper,' Jem said. 'Save your breath for running. We'll think of something.'

5

By the time they got to the bottom, the boys had lost sight of the overseer. They left Daisy tied up and ran for the creek. Jem's chest was burning. He couldn't make his legs go any faster.

At last he stumbled through the feathery wattles, and looked up and down the creek banks. Jem couldn't see the overseer anywhere.

Tommy climbed a tree to get a better look.

'Jem!' he called. He pointed away from the creek. Mr Blain was walking back to the Station. His hands were empty. The sack was gone.

'Fork it,' puffed Alfie.

Jem slumped against the tree. He didn't want the other boys to see the tears in his eyes. He blinked hard at the brown water of the creek. That little puppy had loved him like she was his. Jem had got her out of trouble before, but not this time. She was gone. The Captain had taken another dog from him.

'Hey!' Tommy called out. 'That sack, she's wiggling like a fat grub!'

Jem blinked again and looked where Tommy was looking.

Suddenly he saw the sack too. It had not sunk to the bottom of the creek, as Mr Blain meant it to. A tree had fallen over the water, and the sack had somehow hooked over a branch. It was dangling above the middle of the creek. The overseer must have decided it was too hard to reach.

Too hard for the overseer, maybe. But not impossible to get to, Jem thought. He was already pulling his jacket off.

Tommy watched him with worried eyes. 'This place is no good for swimming,' he said.

'Got a spirit in there, she swallows people up.'

'I don't care. I won't let the puppy drown,' Jem said.

'It's winter,' warned Alfie. 'There's too much water in the creek. I think we should make something to reach it, like a net or a hook.'

There was no time for that, Jem thought. The sack could fall. They had to act now. Alfie and Tommy weren't wrong about the murky water twisting between the banks. But Jem refused to think about it. 'I'm going in.'

'But we haven't got any rope to hold you,' Alfie protested.

Jem pulled off his boots.

Alfie chewed his lip. He looked around, then dragged over a long branch. 'Hold one end of this,' he said, 'and we'll be anchor men on the other end.'

Jem waded into the creek. Slimy mud squelched between his toes. He felt the current tug his legs. He held fast to the branch with his right hand and fixed his eyes on the sack. He imagined the sugar-brown pup inside. How scared she must be.

Jem took a step forward. The water came up to his waist. He gasped at its iciness.

'I'm coming, pup,' he called. 'You're going to be just fine.'

He waded deeper. The creek swirled up to his armpits. He was nearly in the middle now.

He was also at the end of Alfie's branch. He couldn't quite touch the sack. The sack was not wriggling anymore, only twitching. Jem was worried about the pup.

'Come closer,' he told the other boys.

Alfie came down the creek bank, until he was knee-deep in water too. Tommy refused to get any nearer.

Jem reached out with his right arm. 'Pup, pup.'

The puppy whimpered. Jem touched her round shape through the sack. She wriggled.

The sack swayed. It's about to fall, Jem thought. She'll be washed away and drowned.

He let go of Alfie's branch and jumped through the water, grabbing at the sack. It ripped. The puppy tipped out, squirming. She fell in the creek with a splash. Jem lunged for her. But she paddled away madly, with her nose just above water, pointing to the shore like an arrow.

The current pulled Jem downstream, away from Alfie's branch. He couldn't find the bottom with his feet and the freezing water squeezed his chest. He had cramp.

'Help!' he called.

He heard Alfie yell. 'Jem!'

Water was getting up his nose. Jem struggled to breathe. The bank was too far away.

Then suddenly a branch was right there in front of him and he grabbed it. Jem felt himself pulled shorewards. He got his head up. He saw there was a young man in the water, hauling him in.

Jem's knees sank into the mud. He let go of

the branch and knelt there for a moment to get his breath.

Several feet downstream, the puppy wobbled out of the shallows. She shook herself, and sneezed. When she saw Jem, her tail wagged madly. She galloped along the edge and jumped into the shallow water again, landing with a splash in front of him.

'You stupid mutt.' Jem wrapped his arms around her. Her warmth felt good against his cold skin. She licked his face over and over. Now she really did stink, like only a wet dog could.

Alfie and Tommy appeared on the creek bank next to the young man who had rescued Jem. The man was dressed like a city gentleman: he wore a white shirt like the Captain's, a smart necktie, white trousers and long leather boots.

'Thanks,' Jem said.

'Glad to help,' the man said, then he patted Alfie on the shoulder. 'Well done, boys. What's the pup's name?'

'How about Horatio?' suggested Alfie, 'after Admiral Nelson, cos he was a sea-dog too.'

The young man laughed.

'It's a she,' said Jem. But it didn't matter. Alfie's suggestion fitted her. Horatio was a bold, battling name, good for a pup who was always getting into scrapes. Rescuing her felt like a victory.

Jem grinned at the other boys, although his lips were stiff with cold. 'That makes us the troops then,' said Jem. 'Here's to us.'

'Huzzah!' said Alfie.

'Better you come out real quick, Jem,' Tommy said.

'I second that,' said the young man. He reached out to give Jem a hand.

Jem saw the stranger's forearm was tanned and muscled like a stockman's. And he noticed the butt of a pistol sticking out of his waistband.

'Sorry your boots got wet,' Alfie said to him.

'As long as my powder's dry,' said the young man. He patted his pistol.

Alfie held out his hand. 'Alfred Goods, from Ross Vale,' he said. 'These are my mates Jem and Tommy.'

'Pleasure,' said the man. He shook all their hands, but didn't offer his own name.

'Are you going to visit Captain Ross?' Alfie said politely.

'Maybe not,' said the man, smiling again. His grey eyes sparkled. 'I'm not on very good terms with him.'

'Neither are we,' said Jem. 'He kills dogs. He told his overseer to drown Horatio.'

'Bad sport,' the stranger agreed. He was less than twenty, Jem thought, young enough to be an older brother. He was quick to smile, and the way his straw hat tilted was stylish and adventurous.

'So what are you going to do with Horatio?' he asked. He ruffled her ears. She leaned into his hand, then fell over sideways.

Jem knew they couldn't take her to the

Station. She'd be straight back in trouble and so would they.

'She can live with my mob,' Tommy offered.

Alfie shook his head. 'Mr Blain or the Captain might see her.'

Jem didn't want to rescue her for nothing. 'If we could get her to my dad...'

'Better get you warm first, cobber,' said the young man.

Jem put his jacket back on, and the man wrapped Jem in his red velvet coat as well. The lining was silky and it smelt like tobacco.

Alfie stared at the coat and then at Jem.

Jem's teeth were chattering. He didn't care what Alfie thought of him wearing the man's coat. But for some reason Alfie was starting to look jumpy again.

Tommy was looking the stranger up and down. 'I remember,' he said. 'You gave my mob flour one time.'

The stranger frowned at him. 'I don't think

so. I'm not from these parts.'

Tommy nodded. 'Not these parts,' he agreed. 'Up near the lake. You work for that Governor fella.'

The young man didn't answer. He bent down to pick up something Horatio was sniffing. It was a musket. A lot like the Captain's. Alfie backed away.

Jem was looking at the back of the man's hand. It had a small, blue sun tattooed on it. Jem's heart missed a beat. He knew who the stranger was. He'd met him before – the day of the stickup.

Jem, Alfie and Tommy looked from the Captain's red jacket, to the young man's tattoo, to the Captain's musket.

'I'm not going to shoot you,' William Westwood said. 'If it can be helped.'

6

None of the boys knew if the musket was loaded. Alfie didn't wait to find out. He whirled around and began sprinting back towards the Station buildings.

William Westwood sighed. 'Boys,' he said, 'chase him down and bring him back, before I have to stop him. There's good chums.'

Jem and Tommy ran after Alfie. Tommy got to him first. He tackled Alfie to the ground.

Jem caught up. 'Alfie,' he said, 'you've got to come back. He won't do you any harm, unless you try to squeal on him.'

'He's an outlaw,' cried Alfie, trying to break free. 'A robber! He's dangerous!'

Jem sat on Alfie to keep him still. 'He didn't hurt me last time, did he?' Jem argued. 'He didn't even shoot the Captain, worse luck.'

'Jem!' Alfie looked horrified.

'You listen to Mr Jem,' Tommy said soothingly. 'That bushranger man's not so bad. Better than Mr Blain. Not one of them "no tucker for you blacks" sort. He helped Jem from that water.'

Jem suspected that the tucker Westwood had given away was not his own. But he didn't say it. He could see the bushranger with the musket half-cocked, standing by the creek.

'Get up now, Alfie,' he ordered.

Jem and Tommy walked Alfie back, each with an arm around his shoulders. Alfie stumbled along, shaking, barely able to drag his feet towards the bushranger.

The young man lowered the musket. 'Seems to me,' he said pleasantly, 'that you owe me a good turn. I've saved a dog and a boy. Now it's your chance to help me. All I want you lads to do,' he continued, 'is to keep your mouths shut and not blab.' He bent down and scooped up Horatio. 'Since the pup is so valuable you'd risk your lives for her, I'll keep her in my custody for a while. No offence, but I can't trust anybody. Is that a deal?'

'Will you look after her?' Jem asked.

'Upon my life,' promised the bushranger. Horatio licked at his face.

'That your *yarraman* with the sore leg?' Tommy asked.

'How do you know about that?' the bushranger asked sharply. 'Did you find her?'

Jem wondered too. They hadn't seen a horse.

'Saw her tracks,' said Tommy. 'Up there in the bush.' Tommy pointed to the hill where the fort was.

'She only needs to rest another day or so,' Westwood said. 'She'll soon be leaping like a bag of fleas again.'

So that's how it was, Jem thought. A lame horse meant the bushranger couldn't just ride off. He needed their help.

'You better not hang about here,' Jem said. 'It's too close to the homestead.' The Ross Vale buildings were barely a mile away. He thought of Alfie's fort. The idea of hiding a real bushranger there, almost under the Captain's nose, was too good to pass up. 'We know a perfect hideout,' he told Westwood.

'Jem!' squeaked Alfie.

But Westwood had the guns and the puppy, so it was settled.

Alfie walked to the fort with his head hanging down, like he was on his way to an execution. But the bushranger became chatty. He told them that he hadn't actually taken the Sydney Road after the hold up. That had been to throw pursuers off his trail.

Alfie whispered to Jem. 'Do you think a murderer could be so cheerful?'

William Westwood had good hearing. 'I never shot anybody,' he said. 'That's God's truth. But don't tell 'em that, or it will be a lot harder for me to do business.' He laughed. 'Shall I tell you my story?'

'Yes!' Jem wanted to know how Westwood had become a bushranger and what he had done. He was beginning to think that bushranging could be wild and daring. It sounded much better than washing someone else's fine dishes.

Westwood settled Horatio in the crook of his arm. 'I was born and bred in England,' he began. 'My father and mother were kind...' he stopped, and looked away north, like he was thinking of them. Jem thought suddenly of his own dad. It hurt to think of him, working himself into the ground for the Captain's profit.

'They tried to give me a good education,' the bushranger went on, 'but I paid no attention to it.'

Jem was not one for education either. But Alfie looked grave.

'When I was a couple of years older than you, barely fifteen, I was taken up for robbery. The judge gave me fourteen years transportation.'

'You must have stolen a lot,' Alfie said.

'They caught me for a coat,' said Westwood.

Alfie looked taken aback.

'But it was the second time I'd faced the judge,' the bushranger continued. 'So I was sent to New South Wales, to old Governor King's property near Bungendore.'

Tommy nodded. 'Up by the lake.'

'I know it too,' Jem said. It wasn't far from his dad's hut.

'Then you'll know he's a hard man, and his overseer is even worse.'

Jem hadn't seen them, but he had no trouble imagining them as men like Captain Ross and Mr Blain.

Westwood continued. 'He wouldn't allow us enough food or new clothes. I was whipped, for little or nothing. I took to the bush, hoping to make my life better – I couldn't make it worse. I was caught pretty soon by the mounted police. That was three years ago. I got fifty lashes that time.'

The three boys winced.

'But,' said Westwood, with a grin, 'I escaped twice more. When I'd made enough on the roads, I went down to Sydney last summer and lived it up in a hotel.' Westwood laughed. Then he made a face. 'But one night, in the theatre, a cove from my convict ship recognised me. I left Sydney as fast as I could. And back to the countryside I came.'

'Have you been ranging in the bush ever since?' Jem asked.

'Unfortunately not,' said Westwood. 'In April, I was taken again. I was found guilty too – for "being in the bush under arms".'

Tommy shook his head, as if it was all a bit mad. But Alfie looked sad and serious every time the young bushranger mentioned capture and punishment.

'Don't worry.' Westwood patted Alfie on the back. 'I put my wits to work in the lock-up. After a deal of trouble, I got out. And out is where I plan to stay.'

Anyone who'd survived that many adventures, and escaped that many times, had Jem's respect.

The boys showed Westwood the secret entrance into the fort and how to bring up the ladder. Jem got Tommy to teach him the whistle signal too.

Westwood was impressed with the fort. 'This is a sterling set-up,' he said.

Alfie flushed. He shifted from one foot to the other, like he couldn't decide which side to come down on. 'We've got to go back,' he said. 'Or we'll be in trouble for being late.'

'We wouldn't want that,' said Westwood. 'And we don't want blabbing either, hey?'

Jem shook his head.

'Yes, boss,' said Tommy.

Westwood patted his stomach. 'Me and Horatio need some food too, gang. I'm famished.'

Alfie frowned. Jem guessed what he was thinking. Rations on the Station were controlled. Jem and Alfie had no dinner to spare. Asking for more food was asking for a hiding.

'Couldn't you hunt something with your guns?' Jem asked.

'And announce by the gunshots that I'm here?' said the bushranger, sliding the ladder into place for them. 'I think not.'

7

'Can you get tucker from your camp?' Jem asked Tommy, as they came near Ross Vale.

'Maybe,' he said, not meeting Jem's eyes.

'No, he can't,' said Alfie. 'He doesn't want to say no to you, but they don't have much to eat down there.'

'Is that right?' Jem asked Tommy.

'Yeah,' said Tommy softly. 'Them sheep and cows eat the grass, make the creek muddy, so there's no wallabies, no fish. We get real hungry.' He clutched his stomach, pretended to stagger and made a growling noise. 'Our bellies get real loud – louder than *mirigan*.' He laughed.

So did Jem and Alfie, but it was too bad really.

That left only one way of getting food that Jem could think of: stealing. It would serve the Captain right for being a mean old cove. The only thing that bothered Jem was getting caught.

Later, over the dishes, Jem told Alfie, 'We need the storeroom keys. You have to get them off your mother.' Mrs Goods had a set because she was the cook.

That more than bothered Alfie. He was shocked. 'We mustn't do that!' he said. 'We'll be flogged. My mother will lose her job. Where would we go then?'

They could be flogged, Jem knew. Part of him was scared. But the food problem was urgent, and Jem wasn't going to let fear stop him.

'We could already be flogged for hiding him,' he replied. 'We've got to do this for Horatio. A gang doesn't let each other down.' A gang was what Westwood had called them, and when Westwood said it, it sounded manly. 'Tell you what, we'll have a contest. Best man wins. I win means we do it. You win means we don't.'

Alfie picked up a large spoon and tensed for the fight. 'You're on.'

'Nah,' said Jem. 'You already won at slaps. We'll arm-wrestle.'

Jem wiped his wet palms on his trousers. He cleared a pile of plates and pulled stools up to the bench.

Alfie hesitated. 'Stealing is wrong, Jem.'

'Not if we're doing it to help. Come on, just this once,' Jem said. 'Nobody will know. Like nobody knows about the fort. You didn't have a problem with that secret, did you?'

Alfie took a deep breath and flexed his fists. They sat down: Jem on one side of the bench, Alfie on the other. They clasped hands across it.

'Ready, set, go!' said Alfie.

Jem turned his arm to iron – from his fingers, down through his wrist and his elbow and back up to his shoulder. He saw Alfie's jaw set.

For the first few seconds, Jem held his own.

Then he began to test Alfie out. He pushed a bit harder, then harder still.

The muscles on Alfie's neck had tightened like rope. Jem's knuckles went white. Their hands shook. Slowly they began to dip towards the bench. Jem's hand was on top. Jem squeezed harder.

Alfie's fingertips went purple. His eyes bulged with effort. Alfie moved his elbow to get a better angle. Jem felt the shift in his hand – Alfie gave just a fraction, but it was enough. With a surge of strength, Jem pushed Alfie's hand down, until it slammed into the bench.

'Ow!'

'Fair's fair,' said Jem.

'Fair's fair,' said Alfie, although he was very pale. 'Tonight, after lights out.'

That night the boys waited for Mrs Goods to go to sleep. Alfie lay stiff as a board. The wind picked up a corner of the roof and banged it up and down. After a long time, Jem gave Alfie a little push.

'Go on,' he whispered.

'I don't like this,' Alfie whispered back.

'Alfie,' Jem said sternly, '"England expects that every man shall do his duty." Are you going to just spout the words and play around, or are you in it for real?'

'I'm in,' Alfie muttered. He climbed out of bed as slowly as an old man, and crept across the floor. A curtain divided the bed from his mother's. Alfie lifted it carefully and stepped through. The curtain fell behind him, and he disappeared.

Jem waited for a long time, with only the wind to listen to.

Finally he heard a clink in the darkness.

'Got 'em,' Alfie breathed. Mrs Goods' keys swayed before Jem's face.

It was Jem's turn now. Alfie had agreed to get the keys, but he had said he would not steal.

Jem got out of bed. He held the keys tight to stop them rattling. The roof banged and banged. Jem wished it would shut up. What if it woke Mrs Goods?

He reached the door. Alfie pushed up the wooden latch. He opened the door part way, so the wind didn't gust in. Jem slipped through the narrow gap.

Outside it was blowy all right. Metal was clunking in the yard – perhaps the chains on the dray. And that other noise was the loose bucket by the water spout. Jem let the sounds tell him where he was. He couldn't use a candle in this weather.

Most of the food stores were kept in the coolroom. Jem had never been in there. But he knew where it was, dug into the earth beside the kitchen and the scullery, not far from Mrs Goods' hut.

Jem hunched up against the wind. He thought of Horatio and Westwood, on top of the hill. He hoped the puppy wasn't scared. A night like this gave anyone the creeps.

Jem reached the storeroom wall. He felt his way to the door. There was the padlock, big and heavy. He tried the keys until one fitted. The lock was stiff, but with a bit of rattling, Jem felt it fall open. The bolt screeched as he shot it back.

Jem was glad the wind covered his noise. From now on, Jem thought, if he got caught, no excuse would do any good. He could explain being in the yard. But nothing would hold as a reason for breaking into the stores.

The door opened with a *whoosh*. Jem shuffled forward into the blackness, feeling his way with his toes. There were four steps, then a corner, and a fifth step.

Jem stretched out his hands. His fingers ran along a wooden outline in front of him – shelves. He could feel boxes and sacks. But what was in them? He lifted the lid of a wooden box and stuck one finger in a grainy powder. Jem licked his finger and tasted. Salt. No one could fill their stomach with that. Jem tasted the next sack — sugar. No good for Horatio, but…Jem put his arm in the sack, and drizzled a handful straight into his mouth. The sugar was crunchy and deliciously sweet.

Jem heard a rustle behind him. It was the wind, gusting around the door, giving a warning tug at his clothes. He'd better hurry up.

On the ground were several sacks the same size. Most of them were tightly tied, but one was half-full. The sacks held powder too, a tasteless powder that Jem decided was flour. Flour could be made into damper. Jem put the half-full sack behind him on the steps.

He felt his way to the far side of the room. A small keg had a very tight lid, but Jem levered it off with the key ring. Inside it smelt faintly spicy. Jem stuck a finger in, and licked it.

What in blazes! The bitter powder felt like

it was burning a hole in Jem's tongue. Jem spat several times on the floor. Then he jammed the lid back on.

Jem wanted to bolt. But he didn't have enough food yet. The wind in the rafters whispered to hurry. He found another shelf with large, waxy rounds on it. He leaned over and sniffed. Mmm, cheese. One of those would be perfect.

Jem stumbled to the top of the steps, with cheese under one arm and flour under the other. Then he heard voices.

'Mr Blain, good evening, sir.' Alfie's voice blew across the yard in a snatch of wind.

Jem froze. He could hear the overseer's low voice, but not his reply.

Mr Blain was on the prowl. Jem hid behind the storeroom door, and closed it ever so softly, leaving a chink to watch through.

'A noise woke me too,' said Alfie, loud and clear. 'So I came out to pee. There's nobody about the house or the yard. But I thought I heard something in the stable.'

Jem couldn't hear any more of the conversation. He saw Mr Blain's lamp change direction. Alfie had sent him the wrong way.

Hugging the food, Jem sprinted across the yard.

Wham! He had forgotten about the pump. Its handle had cracked him fair across the shin. He tripped and fell hard.

'Who's that?!' Mr Blain's lamp turned back to the yard again.

It was too far to Mrs Goods' hut. Mr Blain would see Jem if he tried to make it there. Jem didn't dare stand up. Instead he crawled under the dray, dragging the food with him. And huddled by one of the big wheels.

Jem watched the lamp flicker across to the pump. He saw Mr Blain's outline in the light. He saw the outline of a whip in his other hand. Mr Blain turned around slowly, searching the yard. Jem pulled his shirt over his face, so his skin wouldn't reflect the lamplight. He held his breath. Mr Blain's footsteps crunched over the frosty dirt. They walked up to the dray, and past it.

'Blithering wind,' Jem heard him mutter.

Jem counted to ten before he peered out. He saw Mr Blain's lamp disappear into the stable. Jem grabbed the sack and darted across to Mrs Goods' hut.

Alfie was waiting at the door. Without a word he let Jem in, then bolted the door behind him. Alfie went to replace the keys under his mother's pillow. Jem got back into bed. He took the flour and cheese with him, because he couldn't think of a better place to hide them.

As his heartbeat began to slow, and the bed warmed up, Jem felt a glow of satisfaction. He had won another small victory over the Captain. He had got what he wanted, and Alfie had had his back all along.

'Thanks, Alf,' he whispered as Alfie slipped under the blanket.

Alfie sighed. 'I don't want you to steal,' he said. 'But I don't want you to get caught either.'

8

Everything on the Station was twitchy and restless in the morning. Doors banged, the wind bothered the animals, and the tops of the gum trees swayed. The stockmen buttoned their jackets and put their heads down as they left the kitchen.

Jem and Alfie hurried through the breakfast dishes.

'We've got to get up to the fort –' Jem began.

Alfie stuck his elbow in Jem's ribs. 'Shh!'

Mrs Goods was coming into the scullery. 'So you're nearly done,' she said. 'When you finish, I want you to bring water.' She inspected the clean plates, and gave some cutlery back to Jem to be washed again. 'What with this wind and all the firewood you got yesterday, it's a good day to wash the laundry.'

Alfie groaned.

'Whose laundry?' Jem asked, as Mrs Goods left.

'Everybody's.' Alfie rolled his eyes. 'The Captain's, all the men's, yours, mine, hers…You have no idea how many petticoats my mother wears.'

'I don't want to know,' Jem said.

'You will soon,' said Alfie. 'We'll have to help: fetch water, stir the copper, scrub the clothes, and peg 'em up. Then do it all over again for the next tub-full.'

'But what about the supplies?' said Jem. The cheese and flour were still under the blankets on Alfie's bed.

'They'll have to wait.'

'What if she wants to wash the blankets?' Jem asked.

'Normally in winter she doesn't,' Alfie said, 'I don't think.'

'I don't think' didn't sound very safe to Jem. Alfie looked worried too. He had dark circles under his eyes that made his nose stand out even more.

'Good thing you're here though,' Alfie said. 'We'll be faster.'

'Let's get to it,' Jem said.

Jem and Alfie were lugging buckets for the first tub of clothes when they saw Captain Ross. He had a ring of keys in his hand. He strode from the kitchen to the storeroom.

Jem wondered what he was up to. The Captain didn't usually do housekeeping.

The boys went into the laundry. Mrs Goods was stoking the fire under the big washing copper.

The next thing they knew, the Captain was there behind them. Alfie squeaked. Jem jumped. Water sloshed onto the Captain's boots.

'Deuce take you!' he cursed.

Mrs Goods stood up quickly and curtseyed. 'Sorry, sir.' She gave the boys a sharp 'behave yourselves' look.

The Captain looked sour, as usual. 'I want a word if you please, Mrs Goods.'

'Stay here and watch the fire,' she told the boys. She followed the Captain out.

Jem and Alfie only pretended to watch the fire. Actually they watched the Station owner cross the yard to the storeroom. He stopped at the door. Mrs Goods put her hand to her apron pocket, where she kept the keys in the daytime.

'You did put them back, didn't you?' Jem asked Alfie.

'Definitely,' Alfie said. 'See?'

Mrs Goods held out the keys to the Captain.

'That's all right, then,' said Jem.

Without taking the keys, the Captain unhooked the padlock.

'You did lock the door again, didn't you?' Alfie asked Jem.

Jem felt his insides lurch.

'I don't know,' he said. Last night he had been carrying stuff in both hands. All he could think of was not to drop it and not to get caught by Mr Blain. Jem couldn't say for sure whether he had locked the door. In fact, he probably hadn't.

Mrs Goods came marching back across the yard. She looked annoyed.

'As soon as the water's hot, put in those clothes. Carefully,' she instructed. 'I have to get the inventory for that man.'

'What's an inven-thingy?' Jem asked as soon as she left again.

'An inventory,' said Alfie gloomily, 'is a list of stuff, like supplies. If the Captain wants to see it –'

'– it means trouble,' Jem finished. Things weren't looking good for him.

Alfie was nervously pulling at his collar. 'Don't tell me you'll work something out,' he said. 'It was your something that got us in this trouble in the first place.'

'All right, book-brain,' said Jem angrily. 'You find a way out of this then.'

'We'll put them back,' Alfie said. 'That'll fix it.'

'How are we going to do that?' Jem retorted. 'And what about Horatio and Westwood?'

'Westwood will have to think of something else.'

But it was too late. Mrs Goods had got a black book from the house, which Alfie said was the inventory. His mother and Captain Ross went down the steps into the storeroom.

'Even if they work out what's missing, they won't know it's us,' Jem said. 'Nobody saw us.'

'They won't know it's you,' Alfie replied. 'Mr Blain saw me, remember.'

'Bloody hell,' said Jem. He couldn't let Alfie take the rap. They had to stick together.

'They can't prove anything as long as they

don't find the cheese and flour,' he said. 'The Captain won't think it was you anyway. He'll probably blame me.' You're not the son of a convict, he thought, but didn't say it.

Captain Ross came out of the storeroom, and stepped onto the verandah. He began to ring the big iron triangle that was used for a dinner bell. It was way too early for lunch. Yet the Captain kept ringing it, on and on.

'Oh sweet Jesus,' said Alfie.

'What?' said Jem. Alfie sounded more like he was praying than swearing.

'When he rings it like that,' Alfie explained, 'it means an emergency or a muster. Everybody has to come.'

Mr Blain was already on his way from the stables.

Jem's mind was racing. He looked around the yard. If they tried to hide anything there, they would be seen. He looked out to the bare paddocks. One of those old gum trees would be hollow, but how could he run all the way out there and back without being noticed? Then he saw Tommy and his people walking towards the yard. They must have heard the triangle too.

Captain Ross frowned. 'Tell the blacks to go,' he said loudly to Mr Blain.

Mr Blain held his arms out wide as if the Aborigines were sheep to be herded. 'We no need you,' he said. 'You not part of the count.'

But Tommy did count, Jem thought. He was exactly the person Jem and Alfie needed.

'You douse the fire,' Jem told Alfie. 'Take as long as you can, so they have to come looking for you.'

Jem grabbed a bucket. He left the laundry, but instead of joining the men in the yard, he ducked behind Alfie's hut. Tommy's family were chatting in their language, heading behind the buildings, out of sight of the yard. Jem put his fingers in his mouth and gave the signal whistle. Tommy turned around and Jem waved him over.

'Can you wait here a minute?' Jem said. There was no glass in the windows of Mrs Goods' hut. Jem opened the shutters and wiggled himself over the windowsill. He landed on the floor by Alfie's bed. His heart pounding, he lifted the blankets. The round cheese and the sack were still there. Jem grabbed them, and wriggled back out.

Tommy was laughing. 'Possum boy!' he said.

Jem laid a finger to his lips. 'Shh! Can you help me out, Tommy?'

'Sure, Mr Jem.' Tommy smiled at him.

Jem patted him on the back. Tommy was good to have as a friend, Jem thought – he liked to fit in with everybody and everybody to fit in with each other. Jem put the cheese and the flour in the bucket. 'Take these. They're for Mr Westwood,' he whispered. 'We'll get them later.'

Tommy took the bucket and gave a thumbs up. He walked calmly away across the paddock. Jem wondered whether Tommy realised the food was stolen. Perhaps he didn't. Perhaps it wasn't fair or honest to put Tommy's people at risk. The Captain would take it out on them if he knew. Maybe he would drive them away, or worse. Hopefully the Captain wouldn't find out.

Jem went to join the muster. He lined up behind the men in the yard. His eyes met Alfie's as he came out of the laundry. Jem nodded very slightly.

Captain Ross stood on the verandah, like he was still commanding a ship. He had a short whip tucked under his arm. He went through a rollcall, starting with Mr Blain, and ending with Jem.

'Yes, sir!', 'Yes, sir!', 'Yes sir!' they answered.

'I will not, WILL NOT, tolerate STEALING on this Station,' said the Captain. 'Not by man, woman or child.'

Jem felt as if the words were directed straight at him. He looked at the ground. He didn't want to meet the Captain's glare. He was afraid the

Captain would see into his heart and know he was guilty.

'Today,' the Captain continued, 'the storeroom has been broken into. Supplies have been stolen. If the thief owns up now, his punishment will be twenty lashes.' The Captain paused. Everyone's eyes went to the whip under the Captain's arm. 'If he does not come forward,' the Captain continued, 'he will get fifty.'

Jem shivered. Twenty lashes was a lot. But fifty – that was the most a convict could be given.

'Mr Blain and I will make a thorough search of all quarters,' said the Captain. 'You are to remain in the yard until we are finished. Now is the criminal's last chance to confess.'

All the men were silent. Jem fixed his eyes on a dead weed by the pump.

'Come on now,' said Mr Blain. 'Let's have this over with. Short and sweet, hey?'

But of course the men were quiet. Jem shot a look at Alfie. Alfie was chewing his lip. He looked miserable. But he kept his mouth shut.

Mr Blain went up to the Captain and spoke softly. The Captain gave Mrs Goods and Alfie a surprised stare. Then he nodded.

They began the search with Alfie's hut. Mrs Goods gasped and looked very offended. Alfie looked like he might cry. Jem wished he could say something without giving himself away.

Somehow Alfie held his nerve, even when Mr Blain tossed their blankets into the yard. A few long minutes later, the Captain and Mr Blain came out empty-handed. They went on to the stockmens' lean-to, and then the stable.

The wind whistled around the corners of the buildings and across the yard. The men stamped their feet and blew on their hands. Mrs Goods began to huff impatiently. She jingled the keys in her pocket. Jem saw Alfie wince at the sound.

Eventually the Captain and the overseer returned.

'One of you is guilty,' said the Captain. 'If

you won't own up, I will make an example of someone at random.' The Captain pointed to the stockman next to Jem. 'Five lashes for him, Mr Blain.'

The stockman's head jerked up.

'Beg your pardon, sir,' he said quickly. 'It could of been the Aborigines as broke in.'

Shut up, you idiot, thought Jem. Can't you just take it?

The Captain tapped his boot thoughtfully with his whip.

'I don't know about that, sir,' said Mr Blain. 'They steal cattle and sheep, all right. But they're not smart enough to open a padlock. That takes keys.'

Jem felt a flash of hate. He despised Mr Blain for thinking Tommy and his people were dumb. But he was also uneasy. Everyone knew cheese and flour weren't bush tucker. He and Alfie had to make sure nobody from the Station saw Tommy with the stolen food.

'Maybe,' replied the Captain. 'Five lashes, all the same,' he ordered. 'Then you are dismissed.'

The Captain turned on his heel and went inside.

9

'I don't like this,' Alfie said as soon as they returned to the laundry. Jem knew he wasn't talking about the washing. The *swish* of Mr Blain's whip was still sounding in their ears.

'Don't growl at me, Jem. I'm telling you honest, because we're mates. That wasn't fair.'

'It could've been worse,' Jem argued. 'Mr Blain went easy on him because the Captain wasn't there. We did it to help Westwood and Horatio stay alive.'

Alfie dumped an armful of frilly cloth into the copper. He chewed his lip as he stirred it into the water.

'I know that. But, Jem, can't you see that

stealing makes trouble? Don't you know how bad it is to be on the wrong side of the law?'

'Of course I know,' said Jem. His dad didn't talk about being a convict, but Jem had seen the scars criss-crossing his back. 'Don't carp at me, Alfie,' he said irritably. He was feeling bad himself for what had happened to the stockman and he didn't need Alfie to rub it in.

'So how could they miss the stuff?' Alfie demanded. 'What have you done with it?'

'Gone,' said Jem. 'Tommy took it. But we've got to move it up to the fort, first chance we get.'

Jem and Alfie did not get any time away from their chores until the next day. While Mrs Goods was baking they slunk around the back of the stables. Then they sprinted down to Tommy's camp.

Tommy was watching an old man carving a wooden spear. Jem would have liked to watch too, but he felt uncomfortable with the

Aborigines watching him, even though they smiled.

Tommy went to a hollow tree and pulled the bucket out. Jem brushed ants off the flour bag. It was emptier than before.

Tommy patted his bare stomach. 'Good tucker.'

Jem was about to say 'the flour wasn't yours', but then he thought, whose was it? May as well share it around.

Alfie tucked the cheese under his arm. Jem slung the bag over his shoulder. Tommy got a wooden *coolamon* full of water, and a bark package full of bush medicine that he said was to put on the horse's leg. Then the three of them hurried along the bank of the creek, where they were half-hidden by the trees.

At the fort, Horatio galloped from one boy to another like she'd gone mad. She cheered Jem up straightaway. There was nothing like a dog for making you feel wanted, Jem thought. It was good to be back in the fort, where he and the boys were kings of their castle. Not a dirty rascal, as the Captain made him feel.

They hauled up the big kettle and presented Westwood with the flour, the cheese and the water.

'Well, boys!' Westwood exclaimed. 'This is flash. We can live like lords on this.'

Jem smiled. It wasn't hard to imagine Westwood as a lord, in the red velvet jacket.

'Did anyone follow you?' The bushranger looked into each of their faces, like he was trying to see whether they could be trusted.

'No.' They all shook their heads. Westwood looked down the hill and over the plain to check, just in case.

'Good lads.'

Tommy started a small fire. Westwood made dough on a piece of bark. Jem tried to keep

Horatio's nose out so they didn't get dog drool in the damper.

'Mr Westwood,' Jem asked, 'how long will you stay here?'

'You want me to move on?'

Jem shook his head. If the bushranger left, who would look after Horatio? Besides, Jem thought, the fort would seem empty without him. Jem liked Westwood. He was bold and friendly and free to do as he pleased, not like Jem's father or the men on the Station.

'My horse is almost good,' the bushranger said. 'Later perhaps I'll push into the mountains. For now I think I'll stay put. If the law does find me here, I could hold them off. For a while anyway.'

Alfie's eyes widened. 'Through the firing slits?'

Westwood nodded. 'Not the best, being on the wrong end of a muzzle.' He sighed.

Westwood moved the dough up high on a rock, out of Horatio's reach. Her tail stopped wagging and her ears drooped. Jem laughed.

But Westwood looked serious. 'Time to check the barking irons,' he said. 'Hold the puppy back.'

Jem did as the bushranger asked. Westwood took the pistols out of his waistband and laid them in front of him. Then he took a pouch from his pocket and removed a small pointy stone, a needle and a scrap of cloth.

'What are they for?' Alfie asked.

'Cleaning. Australia's a dusty country,' Westwood said. He blew on the trigger piece.

Tommy flinched, as if he expected the gun to go off.

Alfie leaned forwards. 'What does that do?' he asked.

Westwood explained: the stone was for sharpening the flint. When the trigger was pulled, the flint sparked against the pan and lit the powder there. The flame burst through the touch-hole into the barrel, and *BAM!* As long as the touch-hole wasn't clogged up. Otherwise, no big bang and no shot.

'And who wants that?' the bushranger said. 'Just a flash in the pan that does nothing, except give the other man time to shoot you.' He gave a short laugh. But it wasn't a happy one. 'I hope to God that isn't how I go.'

Alfie was looking at the pistols with wonder. 'So,' he said, 'the trigger sets off the hammer and moves the cover, so the spark can ignite the pan, which ignites the charge? What a wonderful mechanism!'

Jem and Westwood laughed at Alfie's enthusiasm.

Tommy hugged his knees. His eyes had the same worried look as when he had warned Jem about the spirit in the creek.

Westwood set to work, chipping the flint straight and sharp. Jem could see the muscles of his hand flex under the blue sun tattoo. Tommy stoked the fire. Horatio gave up on the damper and went to sleep with her head on Jem's lap.

'Mr Westwood?' said Jem.

'Mm?' He tested the flint with the ball of his thumb.

'When you leave,' Jem asked, 'could you take Horatio to my dad? He lives in a shepherd's hut near Long Swamp, Bungendore way. She'll be safe with him. He doesn't like the Captain much. He wouldn't mind you dropping by, if you said I sent you.'

Westwood smiled at him. 'I'll do what I can,' he said, 'since you boys are good cobbers.'

Jem was glad. It was the best plan he could think of for Horatio.

'That's in good shape now,' Westwood said. He tucked one pistol back into his waistband. The brass decorations shone in the sun.

'I have powder, for the pan and the muzzle.' Westwood patted the two different flasks slung over his chest on leather straps. 'And I have shot.' He patted the shotbag. 'And we'll soon have some belly timber. I could still do with…' he paused.

Alfie gave Jem a look. Jem guessed what he was thinking – what might Westwood ask for next? It would be impossible to get near the Captain's money or the food store now he was on the alert.

'If you boys can get me some paper,' the bushranger went on, 'then I can prepare some cartridges. In case of a fire-fight.'

'Oh, paper!' said Alfie. He looked as relieved as Jem felt.

'We can do that, can't we, Alf?' Jem said. 'Your mother's got a stack of newspapers.'

'Yes. I can say we're using them to improve your reading,' said Alfie.

'You don't need to go that far,' said Jem. He didn't want Mrs Goods to get an idea like that in her head. Or Alfie either.

'What I'd give for an evening reading by the fire,' said Westwood. He shut his eyes. 'A full stomach, a pipe of tobacco, thoughts drifting with the smoke…and no troopers galloping to the door…' He sighed. Then his eyes flew open, and they were grey and sparkling, as always. 'Newspaper will do nicely.'

Tommy had been sitting on the other side of the fire, watching the firearms warily. He stood up.

'The fire's good for cooking. I'll be going now,' he said.

'Good idea,' said Alfie. 'We should go too. Before anyone misses us.'

10

When Jem and Alfie had dried the last dish that night, they went back to the kitchen. Mrs Goods approved of Alfie's idea to teach Jem. She gave them a stack of newspapers. The Station's newspapers arrived in batches, all the way from Sydney.

'You ought to improve yourself,' Mrs Goods said to Jem. 'There are too many good-for-nothings in this country already.'

Jem wished Mrs Goods would mind her own business. And he hoped she didn't see the guilty look that went over Alfie's face.

Alfie and Jem pulled the long stool nearer the fireplace. Jem took off his boots and stretched out his feet. Mrs Goods' kitchen was probably the warmest place on the whole Maneroo plain. Jem wished Horatio, Westwood and Tommy could be here too. At least Westwood and the puppy had food to eat, thanks to their gang. Jem was proud they had managed that. If it was Jem and his dad who owned the Station, things would be different, he thought.

'Hey, Jem.' Alfie nudged him with an elbow. 'We're supposed to be reading,' he whispered.

Jem held a candle above the newspaper. Alfie turned the page. Jem watched the steam rising from his socks.

Suddenly Alfie breathed in sharply.

'What?' said Jem.

'Read this.' Alfie pointed to the middle of the paper.

The printed letters flickered in the candle's yellow light. To Jem they looked like black ants crawling on the page. 'So?' he said.

Alfie looked at him hard. Jem was annoyed.

Why didn't Alfie read it out, if it was a good bit?

'What is it?' said Mrs Goods.

Alfie looked at Jem, then his mother. His eyes travelled further down the page.

'Um, this is near us,' said Alfie. 'See, that says "one thousand, one hundred and fifty acres" on the river are up for sale.'

'Huh,' said Jem. 'Nice for some.' Obviously the newspaper was for rich toffs. He was even less interested in reading.

A bell tinkled within the house. Mrs Goods got up.

'Yes, nice for some!' she said. 'Why the Captain has to talk with Mr Blain in his study, I don't know. As if I haven't enough to do with visitors coming tomorrow, and now an extra fire to set as well.' Her skirts rustled as she went down the corridor.

'Jem!' Alfie burst out. 'Listen to this.' His finger went back up the page. '*Twenty pounds reward or a conditional pardon...William Westwood, a prisoner of the crown, has effected his escape and is now at large. The Governor directs that a reward of twenty pounds will be paid to any free person or persons who shall apprehend the said prisoner, and lodge him in any of Her Majesty's Gaols.'*

Jem whistled. 'A reward?'

'Yes,' said Alfie, very seriously. 'That's what it says here. A twenty-pound reward for catching William Westwood.'

'That means everybody will be out to get him,' said Jem. 'Not just the Captain, every man on this station. And the other stations, if the Captain tells them as well.'

'Or if they read the newspaper,' Alfie said. 'Keep the candle still.' Alfie held the corner of the paper to the candle. The flame flared, lighting his face and reflecting in his eyes. Then it was gone. The paper's ashes floated to the floor. The kitchen seemed darker. 'They won't read that one,' Alfie said.

Jem was surprised at Alfie. But it seemed to

him that burning the newspaper had not changed much. Although the printed words were gone, the Governor's announcement had not.

'A reward of twenty pounds for William Westwood,' Jem said. 'Twenty pounds.'

'That's right, boys! A big fat reward, for sticking that convict where he belongs.'

Jem and Alfie jumped. Mr Blain was in the doorway. An old army musket was slung over his shoulder. He had a sneaky way of appearing when you least wanted him, Jem thought.

Mr Blain rubbed his hands together. 'We're off on a manhunt tomorrow, boys, on the Captain's orders. Mark my words…' He leaned over Jem and Alfie. Jem could smell his rotten, tobacco-smoke breath as he talked. 'It wasn't Aborigines who stole our supplies.'

Jem forced himself not to flinch. Was the overseer threatening him? Had Mr Blain seen him coming out of the storeroom?

'They don't have the Captain's keys, do they?'

Mr Blain went on. 'But the bushranger does. They were in the Captain's jacket. I'd bet my life he's not far away.'

Mr Blain was wrong about Westwood using the keys, but he was right about him being close. Jem and Alfie didn't dare say anything.

'You stay out of the way, boys,' Mr Blain ordered. 'This is a dangerous business.' The overseer kept rubbing his hands, as if he liked dangerous business, and keeping them out of it. 'You go to bed.' He held the kitchen door open for them, and locked it behind them.

Outside the wind had dropped. A fog was gathering. It crept in wisps around the stables and the lean-to, and pressed up against the library window, eavesdropping on Mr Blain and the Captain. The whole Maneroo plain would be wrapped in it before morning, Jem knew.

Jem and Alfie crawled under their scratchy blanket.

'Why does it have to be twenty pounds?' Jem said softly, almost to himself.

'It's a fair bit of money, I suppose,' Alfie said.

'It's exactly what my dad needs to buy our land,' said Jem.

'Yes, but you don't want Mr Westwood to get caught,' said Alfie. 'And besides, your dad is miles away.'

'If the Captain catches Westwood, he'll get that twenty pounds,' Jem said bitterly. 'When he doesn't even need it.'

A thought had slipped into Jem's mind. It was a thought dark and commanding as a loaded gun. He could not help staring down the barrel of it with a kind of horror.

Although his dad was twenty miles away, Jem was not. Jem had information that the Captain wanted – he knew where to find the bushranger. And the Captain had something he wanted – the land. Jem could bargain with the Captain.

A chill went over him from head to foot. Jem knew the information was as powerful as a weapon. He imagined how it would feel to let the Captain know he held it. The Captain would have to respect him. Jem could go back to his dad and tell him they were both free men. They would work to nobody's orders, masters of their own land. Just the thought of it made Jem feel taller.

'Jem?' Alfie sat up to look at him, even though it was too dark to make out each other's faces. 'You don't…you won't…you can't, Jem, never! To sell him out for money!'

Damn it, thought Jem. Why did Alfie have to figure things out?

'I thought you were all for the law,' Jem said.

'All for keeping the law,' said Alfie. 'But when I heard Westwood's story, I started to think people should get a second chance. I know Westwood has stolen stuff, but you've stolen stuff, and I helped too. Do you think Westwood should be hanged?'

Of course Jem didn't think so. He liked the bushranger, he really did. But he would really, really like twenty pounds too. Twenty pounds could fix his life.

Jem reasoned that if Westwood was caught, the bushranger would probably just be shipped off to Van Diemen's Land, to be a convict for a bit longer. Surely he wouldn't be hanged? Eventually everything would be all right.

'The Captain's only out for himself, or he wouldn't have all this.' Jem waved a hand to mean the homestead, the Station and all its stock. 'If he's going to find Westwood, I want to get something out of it.'

Alfie was silent.

'But I didn't say I'd do it,' Jem added. He realised he had started to care about what Alfie thought. He wondered if that made him weak.

'You better not,' said Alfie. 'Don't say we'll do

slaps or an arm-wrestle to settle it either. If you dob in Mr Westwood, you've broken the gang. No more mates.'

Alfie turned his back on Jem.

'All right, all right, don't wet your pants,' Jem said. He turned his back on Alfie.

But he could not get comfortable. The idea of selling out stuck into him and wouldn't go away, just as if he had a pistol jammed into his waistband.

Then Alfie really poked him in the ribs. 'Jem!'

'What?'

'Do you realise,' Alfie whispered, 'Westwood may never get to court.'

'That would be fine, according to you.'

'No, Jem, the manhunt tomorrow – Mr Blain was preparing his gun. The Captain has more firearms too. Westwood could be shot – here, tomorrow! We should do something, Jem. I've got an idea.' Jem could hear determination in Alfie's voice. 'We spike the Captain's gunpowder.'

Jem was silent. Part of him wanted to stuff up anything that belonged to the Captain. Part of him wanted to help William Westwood. Part of him didn't want to lose Alfie and Tommy as friends, which he would if he sold out Westwood. But he was used to being a loner, caring for nobody but his dad and their animals. To pass up the chance to have land of his own was too hard.

'It's risky,' he said, thinking that would put Alfie off.

'Then have you thought of this?' Alfie said. 'When Westwood's caught, and you collect the reward, what will he do? If you've told on him, then he'll tell on you. And me and Tommy. And what will happen to Horatio?'

'Fork it.' Jem kicked the bedstead. He was so frustrated he wanted to break something. Alfie was right. There would be no reward then – it would only go from bad to worse, for everybody.

'We'll do it your way,' he said bitterly.

'I knew you'd say that, Jem! This way we won't have to steal anything and we won't hurt anyone.'

11

So before dawn next day, Jem and Alfie 'borrowed' the keys once more. They sneaked out of the hut and into the house on icy feet. They took some firewood down to the study, as if they were going to reset the fire.

The Captain was not up. All the Station's firearms were laid out on his desk, ready to go for the day.

While Jem stood guard at the door, Alfie opened the gunpowder flasks. One by one, he spat in them, closed them up, and gave them a bit of a shake. Simple. Alfie was clever, Jem thought, no two ways about it. If the powder wasn't dry, it wouldn't go off properly. Now the Captain's firearms were not worth spit.

Neither was the reward. Jem felt the pain of losing something that had almost been his.

'We've fixed him,' Alfie whispered as they left the house.

'Yeah, but he's fixed me,' Jem muttered.

'That's blood money, Jem,' Alfie said. 'It's cursed. It would never do you any good.'

Jem shuddered. In the silent grey of dawn, Alfie's words had a strange ring of truth.

'There's only one problem,' he whispered back. 'The Captain doesn't know his powder's damp. So he'll still go after Westwood today. He might get Horatio if he catches them by surprise.'

'Not until this pea-soup fog lifts.'

The boys could barely see the buildings across the yard. The paddocks were whited out. The hill with the hideout might as well not exist.

'That's it,' said Jem, realising what they had to do next. 'We'll warn Westwood and Horatio now. Nobody will see us.'

'Let's go to the camp and get Tommy,' Alfie whispered. 'He should come along for this.'

Jem agreed, and they headed to the creek.

At the edge of the camp they stopped and whistled. Tommy soon appeared, wrapping his blanket tight around his bony body. Jem told him about the manhunt.

Tommy already knew. Mr Blain had come to the camp yesterday, he told them.

'We're going to warn Westwood,' Jem said.

Tommy shook his head. 'I don't like all them guns,' he said.

'It's all right,' said Alfie. He explained what they'd done, and why the Station's firearms wouldn't work. 'Please, Tommy? We need you.'

Tommy smiled. 'You need me, huh?'

'Yeah, might be better if you're with us,' Jem said.

'Okay,' said Tommy, 'I'll come then.'

The three of them went upstream for a way,

then they followed Tommy into the bush. Somewhere in the thick whiteness, cattle mooed. It was a low, lost sound.

'I wish they wouldn't do that,' Alfie said. 'It feels like we're in enemy territory.'

Jem knew what he meant. He didn't recognise the way they were going. Without the landmarks of the creek and the buildings the land seemed foreign. It was exciting, but also creepy.

Tommy must have felt it too, because he was singing one of his songs very softly.

Suddenly Tommy froze. Jem's heart jumped. Tommy pointed. A black shape loomed ahead of them. Jem heard the tearing noise of an animal cropping grass. It must be a stray cow, Jem thought. It better not be a bull, not this close. His heart thudded. Then the animal moved. It had a white splash on the dark outline of its nose. It was too slim for a bull. It was the diamond-faced filly.

'Captain's *yarraman*,' said Tommy. 'Mr Westwood's now.'

'Yep,' said Jem. They had come up the back of the hill, where Westwood was hiding the horse. It was time to give the signal. They didn't want the bushranger shooting at them by mistake. Jem whistled.

An excited bark came in reply.

At the fort, Westwood was yawning, and rubbing himself to get warm. His face was unshaven and dirty. Jem couldn't help thinking that he looked restless, like an animal penned up and waiting for branding.

'You're early,' the bushranger said. 'That's good, I hope?'

The boys looked at each other.

Jem spoke. 'The Captain is on to you.'

'What?' Westwood put his hands on his pistols.

'We didn't tell,' Alfie put in quickly. 'They don't know where you are. Yet. Or even if you're near for sure.'

'But they think you stole the food and there's

a reward for your capture,' Jem added.

Westwood ran his hands through his hair. It must have been the grey light, as well as the dirt staining the young man's face, but Jem thought the bushranger looked haunted.

Tommy spoke. 'That Captain, he's getting a real good tracker,' he said. 'My uncle.'

'Didn't you tell your uncle that Mr Westwood isn't a bad man?' Alfie asked.

Tommy looked away from Alfie. His long, dark eyelashes hid his eyes. 'Mr Blain has one of them.' He pointed at Westwood's musket. 'I'm real sorry, Mr Alfie. I don't like trouble with nobody. But…' he shrugged.

But Mr Blain was armed, and Tommy's people were afraid of him, Jem thought.

Westwood hung his head, thinking. The misty air was so damp Jem could taste it. Jem knew what an Aboriginal tracker could do. They read the ground and the bush like Alfie read the newspaper. He realised that Westwood had to leave quickly to get a head start on the Captain. Westwood was a man on the run again.

But at least he was not living under the Captain's boot.

Jem took a deep breath. 'Let me come with you,' he said.

If he joined Westwood, Jem could get the twenty pounds by robbery. Maybe he could even get it off the Captain. Jem knew he would never get to live on that land himself. He would never muster cattle or shear sheep with Horatio at his heels. But his dad could find somewhere else. And if Jem didn't follow Westwood, the Captain stood in the way of his dream anyhow. Without money, Jem and his dad were doomed to a life of taking off their hats and bowing their heads to the Captain.

Westwood shook his head. 'I like company,' he said. 'But with two of us on the one horse we won't get away fast enough.'

'I'll walk to my dad's and meet you there,' Jem said.

'That's a long way,' Alfie said. 'Don't do it, Jem.'

'I'd make it.' Jem gritted his teeth. 'Then we could hide out in the mountain ranges behind here. In summer we could join up with Tommy's tribe and eat those moths you talk about.'

Jem expected Tommy to smile. But he didn't.

'Long time to summer, Jem,' he said. 'Them mountains are cold. That's no good.'

Horatio gave a little whine, as if she agreed.

Westwood stroked her head. 'I'll take the pup to Long Swamp. But don't join me, that's my advice. Mine's a bad business,' he said.

12

Westwood began picking up his things. 'Did anyone follow you?' he asked.

Jem didn't think so, but... Jem and Alfie looked at Tommy. He would know.

Tommy shook his head.

'Right then,' said Westwood, 'you boys keep an eye on the Station. I'll arrange the saddlebags to make space for the dog.'

Jem, Alfie and Tommy lay on the rock and looked out. Damp seeped through the worn patches of Jem's clothes. Everything was still white below. If anyone was down there – owners or convicts, Europeans or Aborigines – they were hidden. It felt to Jem like all the differences that separated them on the Station had been blotted out.

'It's like being at sea,' said Alfie. 'A sea of fog.'

'Pity I can't sail over it back to England,' Westwood said sadly. 'Well!' He shoved his hat on his head, at that same stylish angle. Even now he could almost be off to a day at the races, Jem thought. 'As I can't sail on it, I'd best plunge in.'

William Westwood held out his hand to the boys. Alfie shook it.

'Alfred Goods,' Westwood said with a grin, 'you've truly got the goods,' he tapped his head, 'up there.'

Westwood shook hands with Jem. His grey eyes gazed steadily into Jem's. 'You'd make a very fine Station owner,' he told Jem. 'Men and animals will follow you, if you let them. You'd do better not to follow my wild ways. It's your choice. I wish I could make it afresh.'

Jem looked down at the bushranger's tanned

hand holding his own. The blue sun tattoo blurred for a moment. The mist was getting in his eyes, Jem told himself.

'Tommy – best of luck.'

Tommy was still lying on the rock. He didn't turn around.

'Mr Westwood's leaving, Tommy,' Alfie reminded him.

'Come and see,' Tommy said over his shoulder. 'Watch through there.'

They crowded behind Tommy, and looked down through the shooting slit. In the bush in front, Jem could clearly see the wet leaves hanging heavy on the gum trees. He realised the mist had thinned. The plain was still foggy though.

'Nothing doing,' said Jem.

'Wait,' said Tommy.

They waited for maybe a minute. Westwood shifted restlessly. Horatio whined to be picked up.

'There.'

A pinprick of red showed like a drop of blood on the white plain. Nothing was that colour except the Captain's jackets.

Westwood swore. He grabbed his saddlebags.

Jem hugged Horatio. He buried his face in the folds of fur at her neck. She licked his nose, and then his ear. She tickled so much he had to pull away.

'Hold still, dumb dog,' he growled.

Jem pulled up the kettle.

Alfie and Tommy were still watching out. 'We can see them better now. Looks like they're moving slowly along the creek,' Alfie said. 'I guess they don't know which direction to go yet.'

Tommy agreed. 'They're looking for tracks. Huntin' about.'

Jem hoped Tommy's uncle wouldn't follow theirs. But Westwood wasn't waiting to see. He swung his feet over the edge of the rock, feeling for Alfie's ladder.

Jem put Horatio in the kettle. She tried to get out. Jem quickly lowered the kettle over the edge. It rocked madly. One of her paws slipped through the hole in the bottom.

'*Woof!*' Horatio barked in protest. She looked up at Jem with confused wrinkles on her furry forehead.

'Not far now. You'll be right.' Jem slowly fed out the rope.

Westwood had caught a bag on one of the ladder's crazy nails. He wasn't ready to catch the kettle. Horatio put her paws on its rim and it rocked more. She began to howl.

'*Aa-oo!*' One of her ears had turned inside out. She looked so sad and funny Jem almost laughed. '*Aa-oo!*' The howl echoed all around the rocks. '*Aaa-oo-oo!*'

'Shut her up, Jem, for God's sake,' said Alfie.

'Too late, maybe,' said Tommy.

'They've halted,' Alfie said urgently. 'No, they haven't – they're moving again. At a trot.

They're coming this way!'

They must have heard Horatio, Jem thought. She had given them away. Not on purpose, just because she was young and scared and didn't know better. He cursed himself for not carrying her down properly.

'Jem!' Westwood was calling up to him.

Jem looked down the ladder.

'I can't take her,' Westwood said. 'Sorry, Jem. She'll bring the whole crowd after me. I've got to bolt. Thank the gang – your cut is in the pouch, for being such chums.'

Westwood touched the brim of his hat in farewell. Then he pushed through the bush, and was gone.

Jem wanted to be with him. He wanted to pat the bushranger's horse on the rump and wish Westwood good luck and God speed. He wanted to say, 'See you again, mate.'

But there was no time. Instead he hurried to pull Horatio up. As soon as she was in his arms again she stopped howling and started wagging her tail. He gave her a stern look.

'Do you know what you've done?'

She looked at him as if she was trying to figure it out.

'He's left,' Jem told Alfie and Tommy.

'Not a minute too soon,' said Alfie. 'They're only a mile off. There's quite a lot of them, most on horseback.'

Jem felt a terrible pang of fear and guilt. Westwood had such a short head start. 'It's not Horatio's fault. It's mine. She's just a puppy,' he said. 'She shouldn't be mixed up in this bushranging business.'

'None of us should,' said Alfie. 'Not even Westwood.'

'He left that gun behind,' Tommy said.

Jem saw the Captain's musket propped up in the *goongee* where Westwood had slept.

The musket wasn't all the bushranger had left behind. Horatio was sniffing at a rock ledge where a chunk of cheese sat just above her reach. Beside the cheese was a flat fold of leather. Horatio bumped the leather object off the ledge with her nose. She pounced on it and started ripping at the cords that tied it.

'Hey, let me see that,' Jem said. He held the sides of Horatio's mouth and prised the leather away from her sharp teeth. What had Westwood said about their cut? The pouch fell open. Coins poured onto the ground – silver and gold. Banknotes fluttered down. Three jewelled rings rolled at Jem's feet.

'Oh, boys!' Jem gasped. This was more money than Westwood had taken from the Captain. This was more money than Jem had ever seen. This was the bushranger's loot – their share of the bushranger's loot.

Jem guessed it was worth over hundreds of pounds. It was more than enough to buy the run for Jem and his dad.

Jem and Alfie stared at the loot in wonder.

Tommy didn't. 'We gotta go,' he said. 'That Captain's lot are coming close.'

'No,' said Jem. 'I won't split.'

13

'Don't be daft. We'll be caught, Jem!' said Alfie. 'We've got to go.'

'Listen,' said Jem. 'I've got a plan. We'll hold them off and buy Westwood some time. I know what to do with the loot too.'

Alfie chewed his lip as Jem explained. 'That's going to take a lot of nerve,' he said, once Jem had finished describing the plan.

'Yes,' said Jem, 'but we've got nerve, haven't we? We're not stealing or murdering. We're giving Westwood another chance. And we'll show the Captain what we're made of. Tommy, are you in?'

Tommy nodded. 'I'm in.'

'Horatio, you'll do your bit?' Jem waved the cheese past the black tip of her nose.

She licked her lips and perked her ears.

Tommy laid a finger to his lips. Silently, the boys peered out through the shooting slits, taking care not to be seen. The Captain and his men were out of the valley fog now. Jem caught glimpses of blue shirts and red scarves and the glint of iron through the trees.

'Action stations?' whispered Alfie.

'Action stations,' Jem confirmed.

Tommy climbed quietly down the ladder. His job was to cover the tracks of Westwood's horse. Or at least do enough to confuse the tracks.

Alfie went and fiddled with the trebuchet contraption that Jem had laughed at.

Jem fed the last of the cheese to Horatio. She gobbled it happily, in huge gulps, without even chewing. Her tummy was round as a tub. Jem smiled and rubbed her ears.

'Nice work,' he said.

Now the Captain had to be convinced that he had cornered the bushranger. While in fact, Westwood was galloping away at breakneck speed, putting mile after mile between himself and the men chasing him. Jem's job was to become the bushranger and hold up the Captain.

Jem's hands were trembling as he picked up the musket. He shook its gunpowder flask. The flask was nearly empty. No wonder Westwood left it behind. Still, there was enough for a couple of shots.

Jem measured out a charge from the flask, and tipped it down the muzzle. Next he took a folded wad of newspaper and pushed it down on top of the powder, using the ramrod kept beneath the barrel. He didn't have any proper lead shot, so on top of the wad he dropped in a small stone. Then one more wad of paper. *Ram, ram, ram.* That should jam it – hard enough to go off like the end of the world, Jem thought. The last thing was to put powder in the pan and close the frizzen. Then the gun was ready.

It felt incredibly heavy in Jem's hands. As heavy as death.

Keeping as low as possible, Jem hefted the wooden butt to his shoulder. He rested the muzzle on the rock. He could see the men fanning out around the hill. If they went too far round, they might see or hear Westwood. It was time to draw their attention.

Jem lined up the gun's sights. The barrel was pointing at the red coat of the Captain. He tilted the barrel downwards, to a spot fifteen yards before the Captain's feet.

He took a deep breath, held steady, and pulled the trigger.

Flash! Bang! The powder ignited.

BOOM! Sound exploded through the fort and thudded in Jem's chest. A curl of smoke rose from the frizzen. A grey cloud billowed from the muzzle. Jem couldn't see the Captain's party through it. But he could hear them shouting.

Horatio howled. Jem glanced back.

Alfie looked pale and startled, but he was comforting the puppy. Jem hoped Tommy was nowhere near.

'That'll get them buzzing like bees,' Jem said.

As soon as he spoke there was an answering *boom* from below the fort. Shot whistled over their heads. They ducked.

'I thought you wet the powder!' Jem said to Alfie. The Captain wasn't supposed to be able to shoot back.

'The Captain must have called in men from other Stations. That'll be the neighbours, Jem. There are too many to be just from Ross Vale.' Alfie's teeth were chattering. He hugged Horatio tight. 'That was close.'

Close? Jem hadn't counted on the men firing at all. The shot made his hair stand on end and his knees turn to water. He hadn't meant to put their lives in danger. Now it felt like the Captain had lined the whole world up against them.

But it was too late to go soft now, Jem thought. They had to see the plan through.

'As long as we keep our heads down, the battlements will keep us safe,' Alfie said.

Jem hoped so. The men were still a hundred yards away. He had to keep them at that distance.

A deep voice shouted from below: 'In the name of the Queen!'

'That's the Captain,' Jem and Alfie said together.

'Surrender and come out, William Westwood!' came the next shout.

The boys looked at each other.

'It's working,' said Jem. 'The Captain thinks we're him.'

'By the power of the law, I order you to drop arms!'

'No way,' breathed Jem. He put his hat on a stick and held it up above the shooting slit. He counted to twenty. Nobody fired. Jem took a quick peek out. He could feel his heart thumping against the rock surface.

There wasn't much to see, except motionless gum trees. The Captain's party had all taken cover behind trees and rocks.

'I think they're waiting for us to reply,' said Alfie.

'For Westwood to reply, you mean,' Jem said. 'We can't reply, or they'll know it's not him.'

'They're going to find out sooner or later,' said Alfie. 'Now would be a safe time for us to get out.'

'Later is better than sooner,' Jem said. Every minute was more time for the bushranger to get away.

Jem saw a strip of blue flickering through the trees on their left. One of the men was beginning to move up to the fort. There – another one on the right.

'They're advancing,' Jem told Alfie. They might think Westwood is dead, he thought. He had to slow them down. But not by talking.

'I'll give 'em their reply,' Jem said to Alfie. 'Hold on to Horatio.'

Jem got the gun ready again. His hands were shaking even more this time. He kept thinking about the men on the other side of the rocks. What if, before he could fire, they got so close they captured him, Alfie and Horatio? Worse still, what if they somehow sneaked up and fired into the fort without looking first? The Captain was not a kind man. He would think it was his legal right to shoot Westwood dead. Only it wouldn't be the bushranger he shot. It would be Jem or Alfie.

Be steady as steel, Jem told himself. He lined up the musket through the slit. The sun came out for the first time that morning and glinted off the barrel. Jem hoped the men saw it. He hoped it sent a shiver down their spines.

In the minute or two it had taken Jem to load the musket, several men had advanced at least ten yards. They must realise it was impossible for a lone bushranger to shoot them all at once. The beauty of Jem's plan was that he didn't have to shoot any of them for real. But they didn't know that.

The muzzle of the gun wavered. Jem's hands were still shaking. He couldn't get the sights to hold steady on any one point. He didn't trust himself not to accidentally hit something. If he wounded the Captain it would get Jem in trouble. And to wound a horse – Jem winced. The Captain did that kind of thing; Jem wouldn't. He tilted the gun high this time, well over their heads.

Flash! Bang! BOOM!

The explosion shook the fort. Again Horatio howled. Again Jem waved smoke from his face.

Boom! Boom! Boom!

They'd been ready for him this time. *Ping!* Shot bounced off the rocks. *Ping! Ping!*

Jem threw himself on the ground, scraping his arms in his hurry.

'Cripes,' said Alfie.

Jem crawled over to him. 'I think I've got enough powder for a couple more shots,' Jem said. 'After that, we do your bit then bolt like billy-oh. I'll go first, with Horatio. Are you ready?'

Alfie squared his shoulders and lifted his chin. 'Yes, sir.'

14

Jem loaded the musket once more.

Alfie stroked Horatio and watched.

'Must be a faster way to get a gun to shoot,' he said. 'One day I'll invent something.'

Jem lay flat as a lizard. He cocked the gun and waited. And waited.

He waited until he thought he saw something move. Yes – a man was trying to scuttle up the slope, clumsy as a koala on all fours. It was Mr Blain. Jem guessed he was about fifty yards away. At that distance Jem thought he had a chance of hitting the overseer, if he tried. But he aimed high.

He pulled the trigger.

Flash!

There was no *boom*. Jem swore. Maybe the touch-hole had blocked. Guns could do that, when you didn't clean them between each shot.

'Hang fire!' he called to Alfie. 'Stay back!'

There was nothing more dangerous than a gun that was primed and loaded, but hadn't gone off. Sometimes the moment you put it down, or even touched it against something, it fired, and the bullet zinged anywhere. Jem's dad had told him stories. Jem didn't want that happening to him or Alfie or Horatio. There was nothing for it – he had to get rid of the weapon. Jem heaved the gun from his shoulder, and slung it right out the slit. He heard it crash through the branches.

Boom! Finally the blast ripped through the air. It echoed off the rocks and crackled through the valley. Jem could smell the burnt, bitter gunpowder.

'That's it, Alfie,' he said. 'We're done.'

Jem didn't know whether it would be enough. They'd held up the Captain for about the time it took to eat dinner. Westwood's safety now depended on his horse. If she'd fully recovered, he'd probably be all right. But Jem couldn't be sure.

Alfie grinned. 'Time for the trebuchet.'

He handed Horatio to Jem. Her tail was between her legs and she was quivering. She snuggled into Jem's arms.

'Don't let her get in the way,' Alfie said. 'She could get hurt.'

Jem saw that Alfie had made a line of cowpats beside his cannon. The holey kettle with a rock in it was now hanging from the bottom of the pole. Into the sling at the top Alfie had loaded a cowpat.

'Ready...' Alfie puffed out his cheeks and lifted the heavy kettle.

The pole see-sawed. The end with the slingshot and the cowpat dipped to the ground.

'Steady...' said Alfie, breathing hard.

'Fire!' Alfie let go of the kettle. It dropped

with a clatter. The slingshot flipped up, and the cowpat flew out. It flew over the fortifications, into the sky, over the tree tops. Alfie bent double and looked out the shooting slit.

'I reckon that missed 'em,' Jem said.

'Missed the men,' said Alfie, 'but listen.'

Jem could hear horses whinnying.

'It reached their mounts. Again – quick!' Alfie reloaded his trebuchet. He slung off another cowpat into the blue.

Jem heard more whinnying and the Captain shouting at someone: 'Get back to the horses, damn you!'

Jem grinned. Horses were flighty creatures. They got spooked by strange objects flying through the air and crashing through bushes. He peeked out the slit.

'Do more!' he said to Alfie. 'At least one of their mounts has broken loose.' The more horses bolted, the less men there would be to chase Westwood, Jem thought. He didn't like spooking horses, but today was different. Cowpats weren't going to kill them, but they worked a treat. Only Alfie could have thought that up.

Alfie sent another missile from his cannon. Then he said, 'I'm going to do an experiment.'

This time he loaded two cowpats into the sling at once. When he let the kettle go, the sling swung up with a *whoosh*. For a moment, Jem thought the poo was too heavy and it wasn't going to work. But it did. The mighty double bombardment cleared the fortifications and sailed out.

Alfie scrambled to the slit to see where they landed.

'Huzzah!' Alfie cheered and pumped his fist in the air. 'You should've seen that!' he said to Jem. 'Bullseye! They were wettish ones too.' He added, 'Oh, and they're nearly here.'

'Time to surrender,' said Jem.

Alfie sighed. 'That was the best moment of my life.'

'Quick!' Jem ordered. He was already on the ladder, holding Horatio tightly under one arm. 'Your life's not over – yet. Stuff the loot inside your shirt.'

15

The boys scrambled down the ladder. Jem tore
the seat of his pants. But the seat of his pants was
in for a lot worse from the Captain's whip, if he
and Alfie were caught at the fort. They had to
get away from their post.

Jem and Alfie slithered down into the gap at
the base of the rocks. They bent double along
the wallaby track, through the thick bush. They
crawled under the musket, which was caught on
a branch.

Jem had his hand over Horatio's muzzle so she
wouldn't make any noise. She wriggled madly,
trying to get her head free.

'Shh!' Jem told her. He whispered to Alfie,

'I can't hold her much longer.'

Alfie pointed to a spot just ahead. They could see sunlight falling through the trees onto an open slope.

Jem nodded. If they got out there, the wallaby track could remain a secret, as long as the Captain and his men had something else to think about. Jem and Alfie crawled the last few yards. Horatio struggled against Jem, whining and scratching him with her claws.

When the sunshine touched his shoulders, Jem stood up. He let go of Horatio's muzzle. Now they needed to make as much noise as possible, so the Captain's party wouldn't mistake them for Westwood and shoot at them.

'*Arf!*' barked Horatio.

'Coo-ee!' Jem called.

'Help!' yelled Alfie.

Alfie and Jem burst out of the bushes – almost into the arms of Mr Blain. And not just Mr Blain, but of all people, Jem's dad. Jem could hardly believe it. He stopped in his tracks.

So did his dad. He fell back a step, as if he'd just been hit. 'Jem?'

Before Jem could say anything, Alfie put the next step of the plan into action.

'Look, look,' he yelled. He pulled the pouch out of his shirt and waved it above his head.

'What in damnation are you two doing here?' Mr Blain exclaimed.

'No need to speak to kids like that,' said Jem's dad. But he looked just as shocked.

Alfie ignored them and kept shouting: 'Look, look! We've got the bushranger's loot!'

The rest of the party came running up the slope. The Captain had clearly called out the whole district, including the magistrate from Bungendore. But where was the Captain? Jem hadn't seen him.

Tommy's uncle hung back, leaning against a big old tree. He caught Jem's eye and motioned upwards, just slightly. There was Tommy, half-hidden in the branches.

'You!' said Mr Blain. 'Which way? Where are the tracks?'

Tommy's uncle shrugged. 'Don't know, boss.'

Through the leaves, Tommy gave Jem a thumbs-up. He had done his bit.

Mr Blain turned to Alfie. 'Have you seen the outlaw?'

Alfie nodded. 'We found his loot!' he repeated.

Mr Blain reached for the pouch. Alfie stepped back. Horatio growled and bared her teeth at Mr Blain's hand.

The overseer pulled back his arm. 'Which way did he go?' he demanded.

'Round that way,' said Jem. He pointed in the opposite direction to the wallaby track.

'Where's the Captain?' the magistrate asked the other men.

'Here.' The Captain's voice came from the back of the group.

Jem stared. The Captain's hair, his sideburns, his moustache, even his eyebrows and his fine red coat were covered in cow-poo. Sheer joy rose up in Jem. The Captain had copped Alfie's last missiles full in the face.

Jem looked at Alfie. Alfie was looking at a point somewhere in the sky. He had sucked in his cheeks and his mouth was twisting in all kinds of odd shapes, as he tried to hold in his giggles.

Jem had to fake a fit of coughing. The magistrate, Mr Blain and the men did not know where to look either.

'Ahem – pass that pouch to me, boy,' the magistrate said.

Alfie handed it over, slowly. It was hard for Jem, too, watching the leather pouch change hands, knowing all the loot was supposed to be theirs.

But this was what he, Tommy and Alfie had decided. It would buy Westwood's freedom and maybe their own. Because if the boys handed over the pouch, the men would think they were honest. If the Captain couldn't prove they had helped the bushranger, he couldn't punish them.

But Jem also knew that not all the loot was in the pouch. Three heavy gold rings and a couple of gold coins were missing. He had made sure of that.

'What Devil's mischief brought you up here?' demanded the Captain. Clumps of cowpat dropped from his beard as he spoke.

Alfie looked all innocent and offended. Jem didn't trust himself to talk for fear of laughing in the Captain's face.

'We came up here because there's a good view,' said Alfie. 'We thought we might see where the bushranger was. And we did. The dog found the pouch.'

The Captain frowned. It was a very black frown, with the extra stuff in his eyebrows.

'Turn out your pockets,' he ordered.

Jem and Alfie did as they were told. Alfie

had nails and string in his pockets. Jem had stones in his.

Neither of them had any money on them, anywhere.

'They're not thieves,' said Jem's dad. Jem was glad his dad stood up for him, even though he looked like he would have some words to say later about keeping out of trouble.

'Indeed,' said the magistrate. 'Their morals are commendable.'

There was nothing the Captain could say to that. He might have his suspicions, but the magistrate had declared the boys innocent. They were in the clear.

'Do we get any of the reward?' Jem asked hopefully.

'No,' said the magistrate. 'There's no reward for anyone. We have found the bushranger's hideout, but the outlaw has got clean away.' He turned to the Captain. 'Which is more than I can say for you, my friend. I suggest we return to your Station for a bath and a good meal.'

The Captain gritted his teeth. He turned downhill. Then he stopped.

'You.' He was talking to Jem.

A stab of fear went through him. Had they forgotten something, or betrayed themselves somehow?

'I don't want you working for me,' said the Captain. 'Go back to your father.'

Jem nearly cheered.

But Alfie looked upset. So did Jem's dad. The rim of his hat tore in his hands.

The Captain spoke to him as well. 'And I will never sell my land to you.'

Then he strode away.

'He likes to put the boot in, that man does,' Jem's dad muttered. He looked at his broken hat. 'I wanted to get the reward, to buy our land. But...I'm glad you're coming home.' He put his hand on Jem's shoulder.

Jem leaned into his dad's side. He could feel the

heavy hopelessness in his dad's voice. But there was a nugget of love in it too. Jem desperately wanted to tell his dad everything – especially the last part of the plan. But he couldn't, not in front of these people. He put his face in Horatio's fur.

'Isn't that the ruddy pup from the Captain's stables?' said Mr Blain.

'Does the Captain want her?' Jem's dad asked politely.

Alfie gasped.

No! thought Jem. He couldn't bear to lose Horatio after all this.

'Not bloody likely,' said Mr Blain. 'She's supposed to be dead.'

Horatio growled at the overseer again. She was very much alive and Jem was not going to let her out of sight. She was worth all the treasure in the world. He would give his life rather than let the Captain have her. He held the puppy up to his dad.

'This is Horatio,' he said. 'She's our dog now.

She'll be as good as the Old Girl. But we've got to watch her, cos she'll eat anything.'

Jem's dad ran a hand over her head.

'I better follow the Captain,' he said.

Down the hill, Captain Ross had mounted his horse. He kicked the horse's sides viciously. The horse started forward. But the Captain didn't. Instead his whole saddle tipped slowly sideways. It upended the Captain on the ground like a sack of dirty potatoes. The strap that Jem had worked on in the stable had finally broken. Even Jem's dad turned away so the Captain didn't see him smile.

16

Four weeks later, Jem and his dad came to the Station, with Horatio at their heels. Tommy saw them coming and whistled to Alfie.

Mr Blain and the Captain watched them from the verandah.

Horatio jumped all over Alfie and Tommy.

'Hello, pup!' Alfie said. 'You've grown. Cheese must be good for you.'

Jem grinned. In Horatio's round, cheese-stuffed stomach, she had guarded the pick of Westwood's loot. Their plan had been stinky, but it had worked. 'Good for all of us,' he said.

'But never again,' said Jem's dad, 'or I'll tan your hides.' He gave his son a soft whack on the backside.

Then, with his new hat on his head, Jem's dad strode onto the verandah. The Captain frowned in surprise.

'I came to introduce myself,' Jem's dad said to the Captain. 'We're your new neighbours. We bought part of that big run along the river.'

It was the run Alfie had seen advertised in the newspaper. After Horatio deposited the loot, Jem and his dad had been up to Sydney to buy the land. Now it was Jem's and his dad's, thanks to William Westwood. Just a small run, with a future long enough to last Jem's lifetime.

Captain Ross did not invite his new neighbours in. Without a word, he retreated inside his house and slammed the door.

Not that Jem or his dad cared. Their run included the fort, so Jem invited Alfie and Tommy up there instead.

They lay on the high, sunny rock, with Horatio stretched out at their feet,

'Here's your share of Westwood's loot,' Jem

said. He put a gold ring into each of their palms.

Alfie's eyes went wide, and he put the ring safely in his pocket.

'Thank you, Jem,' he said. 'That will help pay for my education to be an engineer.'

Jem rolled his eyes. 'It's yours to spend on whatever you like, Alfie. As long as you come and build machines on our run.'

Tommy, however, handed his ring back to Jem.

'No good for me,' he said. 'Only make trouble with that Captain. Can't eat it, anyhow.'

'Oh.' Jem was disappointed.

'But,' said Tommy, 'that land we can share. Live on it together. Share some good tucker too.'

'Deal,' said Jem, shaking hands with Tommy.

'What a business,' said Alfie. 'I mean, the whole Westwood business.' And the three of them relived the story, ending with the fire-fight.

Tommy grinned. 'Captain Ross, he looked

like a bunyip,' he said. 'Real ugly!'

'Yeah,' Jem agreed. 'We won the crappiest battle in history.'

The boys laughed so hard they rolled on the ground holding their stomachs. And Horatio jumped on them all, panting smelly, happy dog breath in their faces.

Jem felt the gold ring, hard in his palm. He would never again have to do what Captain Ross told him. He would never be so alone as that first night on the Station. He had more than a run. He had his dad, he had mates, and a pup. And William Westwood was still free, ranging the bush.

The bushranger's boys had triumphed. They were a real flash gang.

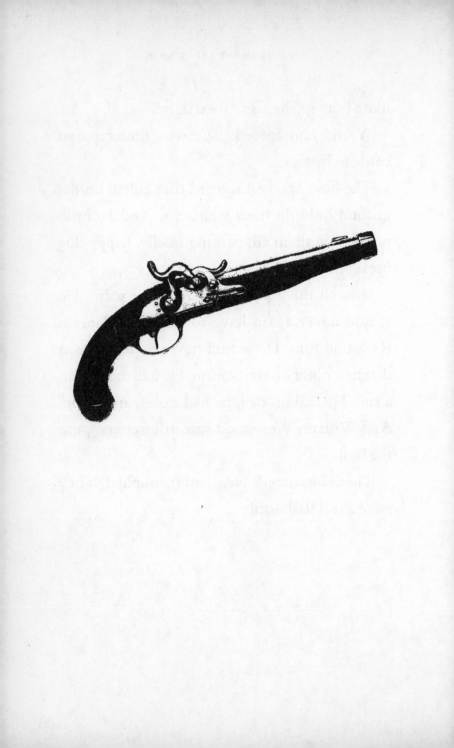

ALISON LLOYD'S ADVENTURES IN HISTORY

Long, long ago there was a Lloyd who fought on the losing side at the Battle of Hastings, in 1066. I wasn't there myself, of course, but I do love castles, forts, ruins and history. I grew up mostly in Australia, in a new house in a new suburb of Canberra, not far from the Monaro plains. Canberra had no castles, but it did have plenty of bush and rocks to explore. It wasn't until I was writing this book that I discovered bushrangers had once roamed the same area, and indigenous Australians before that.

William Westwood, alias 'Jackey Jackey', was a real person. Like most early bushrangers, he was an escaped convict. He roamed around what is now Canberra and Goulburn, from 1837 to 1841. His story in Chapter 6 is much the way he wrote it in 1846, only shorter.

All the other characters in this book are made up. But you can still find the places they talk about. By 1841, British settlers had spread into much of New South Wales, including Maneroo (or the Monaro as we now call it). The British Government gave a lot of the best land to gentlemen like Captain Ross to farm. The foods and waterholes used by Aboriginal people for thousands of years were spoiled by cattle and sheep. But Ngarigo people, like Tommy, managed to survive, and they still have a special love for their country today.

Most Australian settlers had several guns, to use against bushrangers, wild animals and Aboriginal people. Their weapons were slower to use, less accurate than today's firearms and highly dangerous.

If you'd like to know more about Australia in 1841, go to alisonlloyd.com.au.

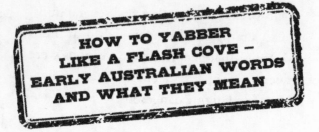

**HOW TO YABBER
LIKE A FLASH COVE –
EARLY AUSTRALIAN WORDS
AND WHAT THEY MEAN**

Barking irons:
Guns – so-called because
they were very noisy and
made of iron

Bolter:
A runaway convict

Cobber:
Mate

Coolamon:
A wooden dish used
by Aboriginal people
to carry water, food or
babies

Cove:
Bloke, fellow

Dray:
A large, heavy cart
without sides

Flash:
Smart, attractive – but
also used ironically to
mean criminal

Government man:
A convict

Goongee:
Ngarigo word for a shelter
made of bark, also called a
gunyah or *mia-mia* in other
parts of Australia

Mirigan:
Ngarigo word for dog or tame dingo

Mob:
A herd of sheep or cattle, or an Aboriginal tribe or family group

Mumugandi: Ngarigo word for bogong moths

Station:
A homestead and farm with sheep or cattle

Tucker:
Food

Yelp:
Complain or grizzle

Yabber:
Talk (in 'Pidgin' a made-up language combining English and Aboriginal words)

Yarraman:
Pidgin for horse

THE BUSHRANGER'S LETTER

William Westwood escaped six times in ten years. He was finally hanged. This is part of a letter he wrote in gaol. It was printed in *The Sydney Chronicle*, on 23 December 1846.

I have to inform you, that long before this letter reaches your hands, the hand that wrote this will be cold in death.

I started in life with a good feeling for my fellow-man. Before I well knew the responsibility of my station in life, I had forfeited my birth-right. I became a slave, and was sent far from my native country, my parents, my brothers and sisters – torn from all that was dear to me, and that for a trifling offence. Since then I have been treated more like a beast than a man, until nature could bear no more.

In all my career, I never was cruel; I always felt keenly for the miseries of my fellow-creatures, and was ever ready to do all in my power to assist them to the utmost.

Sir, I now bid the world adieu, and all it contains.
WM. WESTWOOD, his writing.

AMAZING FEATS AND BIG EVENTS FROM 1841

- The Hunter Valley Bushrangers (known as the Jew Boy Gang) were executed in Sydney.
- The first detective story was published – *Murders in the Rue Morgue* by Edgar Allen Poe.
- British explorer James Clark Ross discovered the active volcano Mt Erebus in Antarctica, as well as the Ross Ice Shelf and Mt Terror.
- The Dreyse Needle Gun was first used, by the Prussian army. This gun was the first breech-loading military rifle, with a self-contained cartridge. It was much faster and easier to use than the muzzle-loading weapons in *The Bushranger's Boys*.
- Edward John Eyre was the first European to cross the Nullarbor Plain, with a teenage Aboriginal boy called Wylie. They walked 2000 km from Fowlers Bay in South Australia to Albany in Western Australia, and nearly died of thirst.

- The first photograph was taken in Australia by a visiting naval captain. The photograph was of Bridge St, Sydney, and is now lost.
- The first children's book was published in Australia. It was called *A Mother's Offering to her Children*.

DO YOU DARE?